Paul Doherty was born in Middlesbrough and educated at Woodcote Hall. He studied History at Liverpool and Oxford Universities, and obtained his doctorate at Oxford for his thesis on Edward II and Queen Isabella. He is the headmaster of a school in North-East London.

He lives with his American wife and family near Epping Forest.

Also by this author and available from Headline

The Mask of Ra
The Haunting
The Rose Demon
The Soul Slayer

An Ancient Evil
Being the Knight's Tale
A Tapestry of Murders
Being the Man of Law's Tale
A Tournament of Murders
Being the Franklin's Tale
Ghostly Murders
Being the Priest's Tale

Hugh Corbett medieval mysteries
Satan in St Mary's
Spy in Chancery
The Angel of Death
The Prince of Darkness
Murder Wears a Cowl
The Assassin in the Greenwood
The Song of a Dark Angel
Satan's Fire
The Devil's Hunt
The Demon Archer

The Sorrowful Mysteries of Brother Athelstan
The Nightingale Gallery
The House of the Red Slayer
Murder Most Holy
The Anger of God
By Murder's Bright Light
The House of Crows
The Assassin's Riddle
The Devil's Domain

Under the name of Michael Clynes
The White Rose Murders
The Poisoned Chalice
The Grail Murders
A Brood of Vipers
The Gallows Murders
The Relic Murders

Crown in Darkness

P. C. Doherty

headline

First published in 1988
by Robert Hale Limited

First published in paperback in 1991
by HEADLINE BOOK PUBLISHING

4

A CIP catalogue record for this book is available from the British Library

ISBN 978 0 747 23505 7

Printed and bound by
CPI Group (UK) Ltd, Croydon CR0 4YY

HEADLINE BOOK PUBLISHING
A division of Hodder Headline PLC
338 Euston Road
London NW1 3BH

To Carla, Grace and all my little detectives.

Introduction

In 1286 King Alexander III left Edinburgh Castle, crossed the Firth of Forth and began a wild ride through a stormy night to Kinghorn Manor where his new bride, the Princess Yolande of France, was waiting for him. Alexander never reached his destination for his horse allegedly slipped, taking both horse and rider on to the cruel rocks below. Alexander's death created a vacuum in Scottish politics. He left no real heir-apparent and the great nobles of Scotland began to jockey for power, each desirous of seizing the throne for themselves. Matters were complicated because the great nation states of Europe, England under Edward I and France under Philip IV, also saw Scotland as an area of influence. Into this maelstrom of politics, intrigue, conspiracy and murder, Robert Burnell, Chancellor of England, sends his faithful clerk, Hugh Corbett, to find out the true reason behind Alexander's death and, if possible, to see if there is any link between Alexander's death and those now desirous of taking the dead king's crown. Corbett is aided by his faithful servant, Ranulf, as he unravels the tortuous mystery in the slums, ruins and dungeons of Edinburgh Castle, the opulence of royal manors and the strange, eerie surroundings of the great Scottish prophet, Thomas the Rhymer, or Thomas of Learmouth.Corbett is threatened, attacked, imprisoned but, faithful to his task, he eventually unravels the fascinating mysterious truth behind the Scottish king's death.

ONE

The rider goaded his horse, digging the rowels of his spurs deeper into the animal's flanks till thin red gashes appeared. The horse, head forward, foam-flecked from nostrils to withers, attempted to move faster, charging the stinging wind as if it was an enemy. It was the darkest, wildest of nights; the wind howled in, almost drowning the clamouring thunder of the waves beneath the cliff but the rider did not care about the elements or that he had apparently left his companions behind. The moon slid between the clouds and the rider turned his head against a particularly savage blast. He thought he saw shadows move there, further back across the cliff, but then dismissed them as phantasms, the product of too much rich food and blood-red Gascon wine. No, he had to reach Kinghorn where Yolande was waiting. He thought of his new French Queen. The beautiful face of a Helen of Troy framed by hair jet-black as the deepest night, olive, perfumed skin and a small curvaceous figure clothed and protected in a profusion of satins, velvets and Bruges lace. He wanted her now; to possess that soft warm body, ripping aside the protests and the pretences. Perhaps she would conceive, bear a son, give Scotland a Prince. A vigorous boy to wear the crown and protect it against the ring of wolves and falcons both at home and abroad. He must reach

Kinghorn and scarred his horse angrily with his spurs. The animal, its brave heart near to bursting, gave its best, almost flinging itself forward along the cliff's edge. Suddenly it stumbled, tipping sideways, and crumpled to its knees amongst the loose shale. The rider, flung up against the dark sky, fell through the night, his fingers clawing the air as he plunged down to the waiting rocks.

'Hugh Corbett, Clerk, to Robert Burnell, Bishop of Bath and Wells and Chancellor of England, greetings. My escort and I have now arrived at Edinburgh, secure in both body and soul, though still exhausted after a wearying journey.' Corbett put the sharp quilled pen down and rubbed the ache in his thighs. It had been, he thought, a terrible journey. He and a small escort had left London at the end of March and travelled by horseback through Newark, Lincoln, Newcastle, Tynemouth and Berwick. The cold had been biting, knife-edged eastern winds, flea-ridden ale-houses with only the occasional luxurious break in a comfortable priory or monastery where he could bathe the saddle-sores on his backside and thighs. His body-servant, Ranulf, had become ill and was left at Tynemouth Priory, and there had been other dangers. Corbett turned back to his letter. 'It may interest your Lordship to know that the legislation enacted last year at the Parliament held at Winchester needs to be enforced. Roads and highways have not been cleared a hundred yards back and twice we were attacked by outlaws. Once outside Newark and again near Tynemouth, by crude fellows with crossbows, mallets and rusty daggers, but we beat them off.' Corbett realised he was understating the incidents: the countryside was plagued by gangs of landless, desperate men. God knows, he, a clerk to the Justices of the King's Bench, had seen such men tried and hanged, twirling by their necks, legs kicking, tongues out, their blackening faces and protruding eyes sufficient warning to any others who tried to break the King's peace. Especially, Corbett thought, after the new measures to enforce law and order brought in by King Edward at the Winchester Parliament of 1285. Edward I of England had now been on the throne for thirteen years and was still eager to enforce his authority in every nook and cranny of his kingdom. Two years earlier, he and his cunning old Chancellor, Robert Burnell, had used Corbett to root out rebellion, treason and murder in London. Corbett, helped by his servant, Ranulf, was successful but the venture had cost him dear. Edward I and his Chancellor, Burnell, were hard taskmasters and had not flinched from sending the woman Corbett loved to a savage death in the fires of Smithfield. Corbett sighed and continued his letter. 'We crossed the Scottish border without incident except for a troop of men wearing the livery of the Lord Bruce, who stopped us and examined our warrants before letting us continue into Edinburgh.'

Corbett broke off to sharpen the quill. Scotland! The men he had met were tough border-raiders dressed in rags but well-armed with steel helmets, boiled-leather jerkins, leggings and stout boots in the stirrups of small but sturdy-looking garrons or mountain ponies. They each carried a shield, lance and dagger, and seemed eager to use them. Corbett suspected that they would have preferred to cut his throat. He did not understand their strange, rough language, though their leader, a smooth-shaven young man with eyes as hard as flint, understood French and carefully studied the letters and writs Corbett and his escort carried, before allowing them to pass into his strange, wildly beautiful country.

The north of England had been a new experience to Corbett who had served in Edward's armies in France and

Wales, but Scotland was something different. Quieter, more lonely, beautiful yet menacing. He had observed it carefully as he travelled into Edinburgh. Vast forests of pine, dark and forbidding, where boar and wolf ruled; wide wastes of lonely, haunting moor, bogs, mountains and lakes covered the land. In England, the old Roman highways, sometimes much broken but their foundations still solid, spread out from London to form the main routes for travel. In Scotland, apart from the King's Highway, the Via Regis, there were few roads, only beaten tracks. Corbett had found it difficult to reach the royal burgh of Edinburgh and, when he did, bitterly wondered if it had been worth the effort. Perched on its craggy plateau, its grim fortress a mile separate from the abbey of Holy Rood, Edinburgh had been cold, dank and uninviting. Corbett and his escort had gone direct to the castle to present their credentials and were brusquely sent back to be housed in the cold, bleak, whitewashed cells of the abbey's guesthouse.

He had wasted two days before writing this letter and was reluctant to continue it for, after seven weeks of travel, he still had little news for his master. He had met the leader of King Edward's special embassy to the Scottish court, John Benstede, chaplain to Edward I, who had extended to Corbett the warmest of greetings. Corbett had liked him; he knew Benstede by reputation as a cleric fanatically loyal to Kind Edward who entrusted him with the most delicate, diplomatic missions. Benstede had a keen lawyer's brain, belied by his rosy, cherubic face, snow-white hair and rubicund figure. Thankfully, he had accepted without question Corbett's explanation that Burnell had sent him because of the crisis at the Scottish court.

Corbett rose, wrapped his cloak about him and walked

slowly round the bare, bleak room. Burnell had summoned him to Westminster at the end of March and bluntly announced that, because of the sudden and mysterious death of King Alexander III of Scotland, Corbett was to travel to Edinburgh and ascertain the true cause of the Scottish King's death. Corbett had cursed, cried, pleaded and begged, but Burnell was adamant. The Chancellor had sat impervious behind his great desk and quietly ticked off on his white, plump, bejewelled fingers, the reasons he had chosen him; Corbett was a trained Chancery clerk, an expert in legal affairs, young enough (was he not in his thirty-sixth year?) to withstand the rigours of a journey. Corbett had war experience, fighting for King Edward in Wales and, Burnell added quietly, Corbett had already shown that he could be entrusted with secret business and confidential matters. Corbett had reluctantly agreed and so Burnell handed over letters of introduction for the Scottish court and to Benstede, Edward's special envoy to Edinburgh.

Corbett stopped pacing round the room, slumped on to the stool and crouched over the small, red-hot brazier to warm his chilled fingers. Then had come the strange part for Burnell had made it quite clear that Corbett was his special emissary, not the King's. He was to report only to the Chancellor, and certainly not to the King or Benstede. No one was to know why Corbett was really in Scotland. He was to write direct to Burnell and only use as envoys the members of the escort who accompanied him into Scotland. Corbett had asked the reason why but Burnell had brusquely dismissed him.

Corbett picked up the pen again and began to write. 'I have met Benstede and he has told me a little of what is happening in Scotland. On the evening of 18th March, King Alexander III was feasting with his court at

Edinburgh Castle, (Benstede himself was there). Alexander suddenly announced that, despite the fierce storm raging outside, he intended to ride to his manor at Kinghorn where his new queen, the French princess, Yolande, was awaiting him. Alexander III of Scotland, ever a sanguine man, refused to listen to any advice and departed the palace, hastening along the road to the ferry at Dalmeny where he hoped to take a boat across the Firth of Forth. There, the ferrymaster also tried to dissuade him but Alexander was insistent and so the ferrymaster rowed the king and two of his squires across the three miles of water to the burgh of Inverkeithing where the royal purveyor met them with horses. Once more an attempt was made to turn Alexander from his impetuous journey, but the King refused to listen and he and his squires galloped off into the howling darkness. Apparently the little party lost contact with one another and the next morning the King was found dead on the seashore below the cliffs, his neck quite broken.' Corbett bit the quill of his pen before continuing. 'Naturally, certain questions spring to mind immediately.

Item – Why did Alexander insist on returning to his wife on such a wild night, braving the very dangerous crossing of the Firth of Forth and an equally perilous ride to Kinghorn?

Item – Why the sudden haste and with so small an escort?

Item – If it was lust for his young wife, then surely he could have waited? Alexander III of Scotland had been married before to the late lamented Princess Margaret, sister of our good Lord, King Edward. Princess Margaret died in about 1275 and King Alexander III did not marry his second wife, Yolande of Dreux, until October 1285. In the intervening ten years the Scottish King had hardly been a chaste man and was accustomed to pursuing women. According to common report he would brave all weathers to visit matrons and nuns, virgins and widows, by day or night as the fancy seized him, sometimes in disguise, often accompanied by only a single servant. He did this on the night of his death. But why? He was no longer the fresh, young groom for he and Queen Yolande had been married some five months. Indeed, there is a rumour that the Queen is bearing his child.

Item – If the King was so overcome with desire, surely there were other ladies of the court who could have assisted him in this matter. Indeed, when he landed at Inverkeithing the royal purveyor is alleged to have said – "My Lord, stay with us and we will provide you with all the desirable ladies you want until the morning light". Benstede told me this to indicate the King's lustful mood. I cannot understand why such an offer was refused and such a dangerous journey undertaken, especially when there is gossip that King Alexander and Queen Yolande were not passionately attached to each other.

Item – It would appear that Alexander made a spontaneous decision to leave for Kinghorn but, if that is so, then why was the purveyor waiting for him at the far side of the Firth?'

Corbett sighed and read through his notes before continuing. 'There must be satisfactory answers to all of these questions and I will try to find and communicate them to you without raising suspicion, although this will be difficult. The general situation in Scotland has stabilised. Alexander left no immediate heir but the barons have already sworn allegiance to the young princess of Norway. She claims the throne through her mother, Alexander's daughter, who married King Eric of Norway. She is only a child and absent from the country, therefore a Regency Council of Guardians has been set up. This consists of my

Lords Stewart and Comyn, the Earls of Buchan and Fife and the Bishops of St. Andrews and Glasgow. I will write again. God save you. Written at the Abbey of Holy Rood, 16th May 1286.'

Corbett checked the letter before rolling and sealing it clumsily with wax. His fingers were numb with cold and writing for so long. He got up and poured himself a cup of cheap, rather bitter wine, and went to sit on the narrow straw-filled pallet of a bed. He had told Burnell that all was well. Yet it was not. There was a tension, a feeling of lonely menace in the royal palace of Holy Rood. Too many prophecies about Alexander's death and, though little Margaret of Norway was the acknowledged heir, there were others with claims to the throne and many more prepared to seek their own advantage in the confusion caused by a disputed succession, not least the powerful Scottish families whom Alexander had kept so firmly under control during his long reign. Corbett swung his legs onto the pallet and thought of the question the great Cicero used to ask about any murder – "Cui bono?" – who profits? Who did gain from King Alexander's fall into blackness on that dark night? Was the fall an accident or the brutal murder of a royal prince, Christ's anointed? Corbett was still thinking on this as he fell into an uneasy sleep.

TWO

The day after Corbett finished his letter to Burnell, he felt refreshed enough to begin his search for some answers to the questions he had raised in it. He used his time to recuperate, chatting to the monks in the monastery, visiting their small library and scriptorium where some of the monks, exempt from the offices of Terce, Sext and None, worked throughout the day so they could use the poor daylight to their best advantage. Corbett loved libraries, the smell of parchment, vellum and leather, the ordered shelves and total commitment to study. He felt at ease sitting at a small desk surrounded by the paraphernalia so beloved of any industrious clerk: inkhorns; finely honed quills, thin cutting knives and small grey stones of pumice for smoothing the white scrubbed parchment. Corbett chattered to the monks, he could not understand their native tongue but many were fluent in Latin or French. They informed Corbett of the divisions in their country, the difference between the Highlands held by the ancient Celts and the South Lowlands dominated by the Anglo-Norman families such as the Bruces, Comyns, Stewarts and Lennoxes, very similar in their ways to the great families of England who served the great King Edward I. Indeed, as the Prior, a tall, austere man with a dry, sardonic sense of humour, pointed out, many of the monks in birth, education and tradition were really no different from Corbett. The clerk could only agree and soon felt at home in Holy Rood, offering to help the brothers in their scriptorium, exchanging ideas and constantly praising what he saw.

Corbett was tactful enough never to draw comparisons or appear to criticise. Privately, he was more than aware of the deep differences between the two countries. There was more wealth in England and so greater sophistication, whether it be in the use and treatment of parchment or the building of castles and churches. He remembered the soaring purity of Westminster Abbey with its pointed arches, trellised stonework, large windows and coloured glass and realised the contrast as he looked at the primitive rather dark simplicity of the Abbey of Holy Rood with its stout round columns, small, deep splayed windows and dog-tooth stone carving above a simple square nave and chancel. Nevertheless, there was an energy and openness about the monks which cut through Corbett's jaded outlook and soft sophistication. Moreover, the monks like those in England, loved to talk, chatter and discuss. The Abbey kept its own chronicle and it was easy for Corbett to turn the conversation to the recent happenings in Scotland and so glean useful information, even though it was based on the gossip of a monastic library. The monks informed him about the court, the current scandals and, more especially, that the young French princess, widow of Alexander III, was still residing at Kinghorn Manor. Corbett decided to visit her and the Prior offered a guide. Corbett gratefully declined this though he did accept a thick serge cloak with a capuchon or hood for, though it was May, the weather was still cold and, wrapped in this, Corbett left the monastery on the most docile cob he had ever ridden. The clerk used a crudely-drawn map sketched out by one of the monks to guide his horse from the craggy plateau of Edinburgh down onto the road to the ferry at Dalmeny. The same route, Corbett reflected, Alexander had taken that fateful night some two months earlier. Now, the weather was calmer; a clear jewel-blue sky across which puffs of white clouds were sent scudding by a stiff breeze. In the distance, Corbett saw the glint of sunlight on the waters of the Forth and, around him, a late spring was making itself felt in the clumps of wild white flowers, soft green grass and the constant chatter of song-birds.

Corbett turned his long, tired face to the sky and for a moment understood the sheer joy and beauty of Francis of Assisi's "Canticle to the Sun". Then he came to where the rutted track he was following crossed another and saw the three branched gallows, each with its blackening, bird-pecked burden. His mood swung in violent contrast and Corbett felt despair, a terrifying sense of the world's sin, a deep malevolence in the affairs of men. "And the serpent entered Eden" Corbett muttered to himself and goaded his horse over the track, across the flimsiest of bridges and up into the village of Dalmeny. It was really more of a hamlet, a collection of long houses built with timber, wattle and daub on cobbled footings while thatched roofs covered both living-quarters and byre. These were scattered round a large green where gaunt cattle cropped hungrily at the sparse spring grass. Half-naked babies played in the dust, watched over by a group of red-haired, green-eyed women. They simply stared at Corbett before continuing their conversations in a fast, guttural dialect. Corbett passed on, down a steep hill which gave him a splendid view of the Forth and the small ferry-port below him. The monks had described the route carefully, adding that the ferry-port was often called

Queen's Ferry, being the route used by Saint Margaret, the English Queen of the great King Malcolm Conmore, whenever she crossed the Forth.

The cob gingerly picked its way down along the loose shale track and approached the thatched, wattle-daubed long hut which stood near a crudely-built jetty. The ferrymaster was waiting for custom; a big, bald, brawny fellow with a weather-beaten face and a perpetual toothless smile. He was a sailor who understood English and promptly agreed to ferry Corbett across the Forth, adding a few coins to the price for looking after his horse and saddle. Soon, they were making their way across the water; Corbett sat in the stern while the fellow heaved and panted as he worked the oars. Corbett nonchalantly asked if he had taken the late King across; the ferryman nodded, turned and spat into the water. 'Could you tell me what happened?' Corbett asked. His companion grunted, turned and spat again, so Corbett laid a gold piece on the board before him and the man grinned. 'It was a raw night,' he said, relaxing the oars and letting the skiff dance on the gentle swell. 'A strong easterly wind had been raging for days, driving the water up the Forth. I was in my house, tucked in with my woman when there came a pounding on the door. I saw from the window that it was two squires, wearing the royal livery, wet and bedraggled, who bawled that His Grace, the King of Scotland, demanded passage. I opened the door and they entered. The King behind them. I knew it was he, large-framed, red-haired, with the eyes and nose of an eagle. I had seen him many times cross the Forth.' The ferryman stopped, smiled slyly and went to pick up the coin, so Corbett drew the long dagger from beneath his cloak. The ferryman shrugged, laughed and continued. 'I went down on my knees but the King bellowed at me to get up and prepare my skiff. I tried to reason with him but the King asked if I was afraid of dying. I replied I was, though more than prepared to die with him.' 'What did the King do?' Corbett asked. The ferryman grimaced. 'Roared with laughter and tossed me a purse of coins. So I got the skiff ready.' 'Was the King drunk?' Corbett asked quietly. 'No,' the fellow replied. 'He had been drinking deep but he was not in his cups.' 'Then what?' 'I took him and his two squires across. Landed them, waited till morning and then returned.' 'Why wait till morning?' Corbett asked. 'Because of the storm,' the ferryman replied caustically. 'One ferryman died that night, Simon Taggart,' he pointed back to the shore we had left. 'His body was found in the shallows. Quite drowned. His widow says that he, too, tried to cross the Forth that night but died.' He turned and spat over the side. 'Poor bastard! He should have known better!' 'So, someone else crossed that night?' Corbett asked. The ferryman shrugged. 'Not necessarily, Simon could have been trying to transport goods. Anyway, many people die in the Forth.' 'When you got over,' Corbett insisted. 'Did you see or hear anything untoward?' 'Like what?' the ferryman snapped back. 'Why, should there have been? No,' he continued, 'as soon as we entered the shallows, the King, followed by his squires, jumped out and waded ashore. There was someone waiting. I heard voices, the neighing and movement of horses. Then he was gone. When I beached the boat there was only the royal purveyor standing, soaking wet on the beach, loudly cursing the King's mad escapades.' 'Then what?' Corbett interrupted again. 'Then nothing,' the ferryman replied. 'The purveyor disappeared into the darkness, I made my boat secure and went to sleep in a hut.' 'That is all?' 'That is all,' he replied firmly and, grabbing the oars, began to pull for the distant shore.

Corbett just slumped in the stern, trying to ignore the rocking of the boat by concentrating on what he had just learnt. Eventually they beached, and the ferrymaster told Corbett where to hire a horse in the nearby village of Inverkeithing. An expensive business, for it was really a rough-hooved garron no bigger than a mule and Corbett felt ridiculous riding it with his feet a few inches from the ground. Nevertheless, the animal was sure-footed. A great advantage as Corbett began to climb up the cliffs which swooped above him. When Corbett reached the clifftop path, he looked round and realised why Alexander had taken that route; with the sea on his right the King had a sure guide along the coast, much preferable to moving inland and be lost in the wild moorlands which stretched from the cliff tops to the far horizon. Quite an easy matter on a dark, storm-ridden night. Corbett looked up at the sky, guessed it must now be afternoon, and let his cob pick its way along while he made sure he kept well away from the cliff edge. He passed the village of Aberdour, where the cliff edge began to climb and Corbett realised he was approaching Kinghorn Ness, the scene of King Alexander's death. It was warm now but, as Corbett felt the strong wind on his face and heard the sea pounding below him, he wondered what would bring any sane man along such a dangerous route at the dead of night and in the teeth of a furious storm.

Eventually, he reached the top. The cliff path was narrow; on one side a lurching drop, on the other a low clump of thick thorn bushes. Corbett dismounted, hobbled his pony, and looked around: the cliff path was now shale-strewn and at its peak before falling abruptly downwards to what he could faintly detect as the royal, fortified manor of Kinghorn. A horse could easily slip and so send its rider hurtling down to where black rocks rose hungrily from sea-washed, silver-white sands. Corbett went on his knees, crouching like a dog as he approached the cliff edge. He ran his fingers along the ledge, feeling the stout weeds which grew along the rocky rim. They were hard, tough, clinging rancorously to life. Except one, half pulled out at its root, the thinning frayed strands of a rope still tied to it. Corbett scrambled back, rose and went to the thorn bushes; there had been someone in amongst them. He could see the crushed, bent branches where the person had squatted. Nevertheless, he knew that the same damage could have been done by any of the curious drawn to this spot by Alexander's death or by the rope, used when they finally raised Alexander's body from the rocks.

Satisfied, Corbett unhobbled his horse, mounted and carefully descended the steep cliff path to Kinghorn. The monks had called it a fortress, the ferryman a palace. The reality was a fortified manor-house, a stone tower with a two-storey stone building surrounded by wooden outbuildings and protected by a huge, long wall and a deep ditch. Corbett approached the main gate and was immediately warned off by the quarrel of a crossbow thudding into the ground before him. He stopped abruptly, dismounted and held his hands up, shouting that he came in peace to pay his respects and those of the Lord Chancellor of England to the royal widow, Queen Yolande. Corbett doubted if the guard even understood, let alone heard him. After a short while, a figure appeared on the parapet above the main gate and waved him across the narrow bridge spanning the moat. The main gate opened sufficiently wide to let him pass and once inside Corbett found the usual clamour and bustle of any castle bailey except for the unusual presence of so many well-armed soldiers all wearing the livery of a white lion rampant, the royal insignia of Scotland. A captain in half-armour, a steel bascinet on his head, inspected Corbett's warrants, removed his dagger and listened attentively while the clerk introduced himself. The captain nodded and marched off, brusquely beckoning Corbett to follow him across the dirt-strewn yard, kicking out at dogs and almost trampling the chickens which scrabbled hungrily for food. They passed open kitchens, stables and a forge with their blackened, perspiring servants, entered the main building and climbed steep stone stairs. At the top the guard captain tapped lightly on a steel-studded door. A soft voice called "Entrez!" and Corbett was shown into a small though luxurious chamber with velvet buckram drapes on the walls, soft herb-strewn rushes on the floor with small, scented braziers placed around the walls. In the centre of the room was a woman sitting regally in a beautiful carved wooden chair, studying a piece of parchment in her lap. A group of ladies sat a fair distance away beneath the room's one and only window, ostensibly embroidering a piece of tapestry stretched across a stand.

The captain went down on one knee and muttered an introduction in atrocious French. The woman in the chair looked up, stared at him and then Corbett. Queen Yolande was beautiful with a small oval face, her skin was a tawny gold, her nose small, the eyes large and darkened. Only her mouth, pert and rather pouting, marred the effect for she looked arrogant and rather spoilt. Her dress was black silk though Corbett noticed that it emphasised rather than hid her plump breasts and narrow waist, and the white fox-fur on the cuffs of her gown drew attention to her fine wrists and long, white, bejewelled fingers. She chattered to the captain in French, dismissed him and beckoned Corbett to a small stool in front of her. Corbett felt slightly ridiculous and heard subdued laughter from one of her ladies, a rather overblown red-head, likewise in black, who was in the centre of the group involved with the tapestry.

The laughter was silenced by an imperious glance from Queen Yolande before she turned to question Corbett in French. He courteously replied, tactfully lying about his arrival in Scotland and explaining that he came with the personal condolences of the Lord Chancellor of England. Queen Yolande heard him out though she appeared to be only half listening. Gently, Corbett turned the conversation to the death of her husband. 'It is a pity, my Lady,' Corbett commented politely, 'that His Grace should have attempted that journey on such a wild night!' He bowed graciously towards her. 'I realise you are still in mourning and the subject is most painful to you, but the thought did occur to me as I made the same journey today.' The royal widow simply shrugged her elegant shoulders. 'His Grace was always impetuous!' she almost snapped. 'He should not have travelled in such rough weather. I could scarcely believe the message he sent earlier that day saying he would come!' 'His Grace told you that he was coming that night?' Corbett tentatively asked. 'When did he send such a message?' 'What business is it of yours?' Yolande snapped back, staring hard at Corbett. 'A messenger delivered a letter later that day. I don't know who brought it! I only remember because I immediately burnt it in exasperation!' Corbett smiled understandingly and gently diverted the conversation to other matters. He had asked enough questions and was sufficiently startled by Yolande to conceal his feelings behind the mask of diplomacy. He felt uneasy. Yolande was a royal widow; in a sense, her husband's passion for her had caused his death; yet Yolande seemed to resent, even hate her dead husband. Was this the woman, Corbett wondered, who had drawn King Alexander III of Scotland to gamble his life for her? Corbett could not pinpoint or express his reasons for the conclusions he drew but he felt the unease, something insubstantial, like a perfume emanating from this spoilt beautiful woman.

Corbett allowed the now desultory conversation to continue before discreetly interrupting. 'Madam, my master and His Grace, King Edward, will be delighted with the news that you are "enceinte". A small consolation at this time of great sorrow ...' Yolande almost smirked as she gently patted her stomach. 'I do not care for your King, Master Corbett, but, yes, I do care for a possible future King of Scotland!' Corbett heard a snort of laughter from the red-headed lady-in-waiting, but ignored it. Queen Yolande did not. She spun round, glared at the woman and turned back to extend her hand to Corbett as a sign that the audience was over. Corbett bent, kissed the Queen's cool white hand and withdrew, ignoring the brazen look of the lady-in-waiting who had brought his interview to such a sudden end.

THREE

Outside the chamber, Corbett found the captain of the guard waiting for him, a little more relaxed now he realised that Corbett was acceptable to the Queen-Dowager. 'Are you intent on leaving this evening?' he asked, his English accent thick and guttural. 'Why?' Corbett smiled at him. 'Do I have a choice?' The soldier shrugged. 'You may stay and catch the ferry at first light when it crosses but that is your decision.' 'Then thank you,' Corbett courteously replied, 'I will stay. But tell me,' he added. 'Who is the red-headed lady-in-waiting to the Queen? She seemed a brazen hussy!' Now the soldier smiled, a yellow-toothed grin cracking the severity of his face. 'You mean Agnes Lennox?' he jibed. 'You're right. A brazen hussy indeed. There is no love lost between her and the Queen. Why?' 'Nothing,' Corbett muttered. 'But, look. Were you on duty the night the King died?' 'Of course. Though I never stirred from here. News of his death was brought by a messenger.' 'The same messenger,' Corbett interjected, 'who brought you news that the King intended to travel to Kinghorn?' 'Whish, no, man,' the soldier replied. 'That was simply a letter delivered at the gate just before dusk. God knows who brought it. You had best ask the purveyor that question.' Corbett felt his heart quicken. 'The same purveyor who greeted the King when he landed from the ferry?' 'Oh, aye,' the soldier replied. 'Alexander, he has the same name as the late king. Why do you ask?' he narrowed his eyes and stared hard at Corbett. 'You ask a lot of questions, Master Clerk, from England!' Corbett smiled. 'I am sorry,' he apologised. 'But the English court were so shocked by the death of your king they could scarcely believe it. My masters expect me to be hunting for news.' The soldier relaxed and tapped Corbett patronisingly on the shoulder. 'Yes, I know. We are all under orders. I can scarcely believe the King is dead and think it just a rumour. But, come, I will introduce you to Alexander, he's told his story many times. I vow he'd love to tell it again.'

Corbett followed the captain down the winding stone staircase and into the main hall. In happier, better times it may have looked princely, even regal, with the raised dais at the far end under a huge tapestry emblazoned with the royal insignia of Scotland. Now it was dingy. The rushes on the floor were none too clean: hungry wolf-hounds foraged amongst them for bits of food and Corbett heard the squeak and scamper of rats. The trestle tables down each side were stained with wine and strewn with the stale remains of various meals. On the walls, the cresset torches, untended, spluttered fiercely in their sconces and Corbett realised that the retainers were taking full advantage of a dead king and his lonely, isolated widow. At the end of one table sat a group of men surrounded by cups and flagons, rolling a set of dice amidst curses and shouts. The captain took Corbett by the sleeve, led him over to them and tapped one of the players on the shoulder. 'Alexander,' he taunted. 'Here's a man who would like to hear your story!' Alexander turned, a long, horsy face, bulbous blue eyes and wet slack mouth beneath a shock of black hair. 'I'm at dice!' he grumbled and glared angrily at Corbett. 'I know,' the English clerk sweetly replied, 'but,' and he jingled the coins in his purse. 'I can make up your undoubted losses!' Alexander was too far gone in his cups to detect the sarcasm but he looked at Corbett, licked his lips greedily and, snatching up a brimming cup, lurched to his feet and gestured Corbett to follow him to the far end of the room. The captain of the guard nodded at Corbett to follow and promptly occupied the gambler's vacant seat. 'Oh,' he shouted after Corbett. 'When he's finished his tale, just bed down here in the hall. I will bring you a cloak, it is not much, but warmer and more comfortable than a night on the cliff tops!' Corbett nodded, smiled his thanks and went over to where Alexander now slouched in a half-drunken stupor.

Corbett introduced himself, giving the same reason for his curiosity as he had earlier. Alexander was too drunk to care and Corbett had to listen carefully to understand the man's drunken, slurred speech. Like himself, Alexander was a clerk who served the King, even following him to England when the late Scottish King had gone south to attend the coronation of Edward I. Corbett let him ramble on while the gambling group broke up amidst loud shouts and farewells, and a harassed servant brought Corbett a cloak. Then the English clerk gently asked the befuddled Alexander his questions, though he learnt nothing new. On the day the King died, just before dusk, an unknown messenger had delivered a letter at the gate. This was taken direct to Queen Yolande who had summoned Alexander and told him to take the King's favourite horse, a white mare stabled at Kinghorn, down to the ferry. Alexander angrily complied, furious that the King could put him to so much trouble on a wild, bitterly cold night. 'I did what I was told to,' he grumbled. 'I waited there for hours until His Grace came. I remonstrated with him but he would not listen. He had to be with the Queen and so he rode off.' 'And what did you do?' Alexander belched and scratched his chin. 'I went to a tavern in Inverkeithing where I was joined by one of the King's squires.' 'You what?' Corbett asked. 'One of the King's companions?' 'The same,' Alexander replied, trying to focus on this curious English clerk. 'The poor bastard was thrown by his horse and had to walk back to the village. We both stayed there till late the following day.' He looked slyly at Corbett. 'You see, we were drinking. It was only when we left the tavern that we heard about the King.' Corbett nodded and pushed a few coins into the purveyor's slack hands. 'So, who found the King's body?' 'Oh, a party from the castle across the Forth, they gathered it up and it was taken back on a royal barge.' Corbett nodded understandingly while he concentrated on listing a sequence of events surrounding the Scottish King's death. There was something wrong, very wrong but he could not grasp it. 'Tell me,' he said slowly. 'One squire stayed with you? And he never reached the manor?' Alexander nodded. 'So what happened to the other one?' Corbett continued. 'If he reached the manor, why did he not come back to look for his master? In fact,' Corbett now tried to clear the doubts in his own mind, 'why didn't the Queen send out a search-party for her husband? After all, he was expected?' The purveyor stared hard at the table, as he tried to concentrate. 'I don't know,' he muttered. 'The fellow who stayed with me went back and so did the other squire. He evidently rode ahead of the King and reached the manor. Why he or the Queen never thought of searching for the King is a mystery.' He stared drunkenly at Corbett. 'The whole thing's a mystery, Master Clerk, and perhaps you should answer questions. The King's desire to join the Queen is a mystery, for,' he added bitterly, 'he would have had little joy out of her.' 'What do you mean?' Corbett asked. 'Did Queen Yolande hate her husband?' Alexander only grimaced, farted, then fell head forward into a drunken sleep. Corbett cursed and rose to his feet. He took the dirty threadbare cloak and, finding the cleanest spot in the hall, lay down and fell asleep.

The next morning Corbett woke, feeling dirty and aching in every joint. He got up, went out into the courtyard to piss and onto the kitchen to beg for a cup of watered ale and a slice of greasy bacon to silence the hunger pangs of his stomach for he had not eaten since leaving Holy Rood Abbey the previous day. Corbett wanted to leave Kinghorn quickly before the captain or Alexander began to question him, so, once he had finished his meal, he went to the stable and, saddling the garron, led him out towards the main gate. Corbett was almost there when he heard a voice call out. He turned and saw the red-haired Lennox woman coming out of the door of the main building, an earthenware jar in her hand. Corbett quietly groaned and stopped as she approached. 'Are ye leaving so soon, Master English Clerk?' she asked suggestively, her eyes boldly studying Corbett from head to toe. 'Yes, I'm leaving,' the clerk replied. 'I have to. Perhaps next time?' 'Next time,' Agnes whispered huskily, 'we must talk, become better acquainted?' 'Yes,' Corbett replied, 'but not now! Goodbye!' 'Till then, Master Clerk,' came the brazen reply. 'Till the next time!' Corbett sighed, turned his horse and, after a short argument with a sleepy guard, left Kinghorn for the ferry.

He reached it without mishap but had to wait for a while, watching the day begin, until the ferrymaster arrived. He greeted Corbett warmly, ensured that the garron was safely returned to its stable in Inverkeithing and then rowed Corbett out across the Forth. This time, he asked the questions, curious about the Queen and the doings of the great ones of the land. Corbett, cold and hungry, muttered his replies and was more than pleased when they reached Queensferry. Corbett was just about to leave to collect his cob from the stables when he remembered something and hurried back to the ferrymaster. 'Tell me,' he urged, 'did you take anyone else across the Forth the day the King died?' The ferrymaster shook his head. 'Na, na,' he replied. 'The storm lasted all day. I only took the King!' 'But somebody must have?' Corbett asked testily. 'Aye. Maybe they did,' the ferrymaster replied. 'But it was not me!' 'Who then?' The ferrymaster grinned. 'Taggart. Perhaps. But he is dead. Isn't he?' Corbett turned angrily on his heel, collected the cob and wearily made his way back to the Abbey of Holy Rood.

Corbett did not go through Edinburgh but took the same route as he had earlier followed, skirting the city, plodding his way through marsh and bog till he reached the clean, white sanctity of the Abbey. The Prior welcomed him sardonically but Corbett could see the monks were genuinely pleased to see him back. For the first time for a long while, Corbett felt wanted and warmed to these simple yet sophisticated men so bound up in their own routine of prayer, work and study that they regarded any visitor as a visible sign of God's grace. They questioned him about his journey, about Kinghorn and Queen Yolande, until the Prior intervened, pointing out that their visitor needed to relax.

Corbett bathed in the guest-house's one and only tub before dressing and going down to the buttery for ale and a bowl of bread and fish boiled in milk. He then went to the library. It was now dusk but the old librarian had the sconce torches lit and gave Corbett what he had requested, a candle and a battered copy of the "Sic et Non', the brilliant satire on scholastic theology by the Parisian scholar, Abelard, who had lost his family as well as his testicles for ridiculing the theologians and then compounding his sin by falling in love with a woman. Corbett loved the brilliant logic delivered so tongue-in-cheek that only those who wished to take offence would be affronted. He read it carefully, the lucid language and poetry of argument clearing and settling his mind. Darkness fell. The librarian, fearful of fire, gently shooed Corbett out so the clerk went down to stroll in the monastery's small herb garden while he rigorously analysed all he had learnt in his journey to Kinghorn. Corbett walked and argued with himself until the bells tolling for Compline brought him into the Abbey church with its lofty roof, pointed arches and round drum-like columns. He went up the nave and into the square chancel where the monks were gathered, seated in benches on each side. The main cantor rose and began the prayer, warning the brothers that Satan roamed the world like a starving lion looking for victims he could devour. Corbett, gently dreaming at the end of a bench, could well believe it and wondered if this time Satan would search him out.

FOUR

Satan did walk Scotland and no more so than in the chambers and corridors of Edinburgh Castle. King Alexander was dead. His body now lay rotting under the cold grey slabs of an abbey, his strong rule was gone and, throughout the castle, nobles gathering for the council plotted and intrigued. Friendships died, new alliances were made and old ones betrayed as the powerful barons, courtiers and important officials scented the power, influence and wealth now available for the throne was empty with no real heir-apparent. Alexander had kept them leashed, curbed and checked, but now the leading nobles were almost drunk with a feeling of power and freedom.

In his own chamber, the Lord Bruce showed these feelings but he was a practical man who simply believed power should be grasped and wielded. He sat, a wine cup clenched firmly in his hands, as he stared through a window into the gathering darkness. The King was dead. Thank God he was, Bruce thought! Adulterer! Lecher! A good warrior but the Bruces had as much claim to Alexander's throne as he had, and now the throne was empty. Bruce stirred and wrapped his cloak firmly about him. There would be confusion, Bruce thought, and out of this a strong ruler would need to emerge. A man fit to rule with an iron hand, to hold down the wild men of the North, the seafarers of the isles and the wealthy Norman barons in the south. Bruce was glad Alexander was dead. He felt guilty at the thoughts which flooded into his mind. He would need to confess them, be shrived, for even to think about the King's death was treason. For a short while, Bruce's mind wondered what measure of guilt he bore, for had he not wished the King's death? Almost danced with joy as the royal corpse was brought back from Kinghorn? He should hide such thoughts for they could well call Alexander back from Hell to exact his vengeance.

In other chambers men, lords and their retainers sat and gossiped about what would happen next. Alexander had left an heir, a weak baby princess, living in the Norwegian court. But was she fit to rule? And who else was there? The Comyns? The Balliols? And, of course, Edward of England. Bishop Wishart, Chancellor of Scotland, also considered these names. He sat at his desk, huddled in his great cloak, oblivious to the cold draughts which came under the door or through the cracks in the wooden shutters on the window. Candles in iron candelabra shed some light but Wishart preferred the darkness, even the cold, so he could think clearly, logically, plan and plot.

Wishart had one great love, Scotland. He did not mind who ruled the kingdom as long as the prince was strong, courageous and ready to defend it against a ring of enemies. Wishart was an educated man. He had travelled over Europe and had witnessed what was happening. The great kings, Philip of France and Edward of England, were building up nation states. Roads were being levelled, armies raised, castles erected, laws passed, justice imposed, while Scotland was still a collection of races. Only an iron clasp, the steel hand of a ruthless king would keep them in check and create peace throughout the country.

Wishart secretly mourned Alexander. He had not liked the man. The dead King had been a lecher who lusted after other men's wives, daughters, sisters, like a dog on heat. Nevertheless, Alexander had been strong. Now he was gone, suddenly and mysteriously. Wishart stirred restlessly. Should he examine that problem? God knows there were many who wanted Alexander dead. The Bruces, the Comyns. The men whose women had been his mistresses. They all had their motives. Wishart narrowed his eyes and looked into the candlelight. There had been rumours, warnings about Alexander's death long before it happened. In this castle, months before the tragedy, there had been a banquet. Alexander was there surrounded by his mistresses and friends, drinking and eating. Wishart had been away but he had heard the stories later, how Alexander had suddenly looked down the hall, dropping his cup and going pale with fright. "What is it my Lord?" courtiers had asked. Alexander shook his head, and, raising his hand, pointed down into the darkness. "I see a man," he replied softly. "A monk. A man in a shroud. Can't you see him?" "No, my Lord," came the reply. Alexander had continued to stare, completely sober now, at the apparition only he could see. "He is warning me about my death," Alexander announced quietly, "Violent and soon to happen!" The alleged vision had spoiled the banquet, depressed the King for weeks afterwards, before his natural good-humour and boisterous spirits dismissed it as a phantasm of too much drink.

Wishart bit his lip. He did not trust in visions. He did not believe God had the time to interfere in the petty affairs of men. Was it some trick of the light? Or had someone planted the idea in Alexander's mind? There were other mysterious happenings. The prophecies of Thomas the Rhymer, or Thomas of Learmouth, the self-proclaimed seer, who claimed he had dreams of Alexander's death, constantly warning the King of this in four-line doggerel verse. Wishart grunted. One day his inquisitors would take Master Learmouth and put him to the question. Was he a prophet? Or a man who meddled in the black arts? Whatever, his prophecies about Alexander's death had been proven brutally correct.

Wishart felt as if he was standing at a crossroads with two paths leading into the darkness. On the left, the problem of solving the King's death, of finding the murderer. On the right, the even more pressing problem of who was to succeed Alexander. The barons had sworn to uphold the cause of his granddaughter in Norway, but could a three-year-old girl rule Scotland? Or would it be someone else? Perhaps if he followed one path, he would find a place where they came together? Perhaps Alexander was not murdered, perhaps it was an accident. Perhaps the result of jealousy, some man sickened and tired of the king seducing or pursuing a woman. Yet, there could be other reasons. Did one of the claimants to the throne arrange the murder?

Wishart had considered Edward of England but then dismissed him. Edward was in France. There was no sign of his meddling in Scottish affairs, apart from sending his envoy, Benstede, and that inquisitive clerk, Corbett, across the border. Benstede had been there before Alexander died and Corbett, so Wishart's spies told him, was not sent by the King but the Chancellor of England, that wily old fox, Robert Burnell. Wishart had Corbett watched carefully but all the reports indicated that Corbett had not been officially despatched by Edward. Wishart quietly wondered what was happening in the English court. Perhaps there was a division? Nevertheless, the bishop was firmly assured that, as yet, the English posed no threat.

Wishart rose and crossed the darkened chamber to secure one of the wooden shutters. He turned and warmed his hands over a small charcoal brazier. The French, he thought, were a different matter; their envoy, de Craon, was already in Scotland, plotting and conspiring with that bitch of a widow-queen. Wishart rubbed his hands together, cracking his knuckles as he tried to control his anger. He had never liked Queen Yolande with her haughty airs and fastidious manner, locking herself up at Kinghorn Manor and keeping away from the King. Alexander was, allegedly, infatuated with her but there was something wrong. She was supposed to be pregnant and perhaps Scotland might still get its heir but would it be a male prince and who would protect him over the coming years? Wishart sighed deeply. Then, of course, there were the Bruces, Lord Bruce who should be preparing himself for death instead of being involved in politics as if he were some young courtier intent on rising as fast and as far as he could.

Wishart thought back to what he had heard about that fateful night at the banquet. Bruce had been there, so had the English and French envoys. De Craon had looked upset. Benstede, impassive, had left early, while Bruce scarcely bothered to disguise the murder in his eyes whenever he caught the King's glance. The King had been so glum on his arrival and then, suddenly, almost out of character even for him, his mood had changed to one of enjoyment, drinking deeply, boasting that he would be with the Queen before the night was out, then off riding into that terrible storm to his death on the top of Kinghorn Cliff. Was someone there waiting for him, Wishart thought? No. No one at the banquet could possibly have crossed the Firth of Forth in such weather with such speed and he knew from his own spies that only the King had crossed the Forth that night. Deep in his heart Wishart believed the King had been murdered but he did not know how, or why, or by whom. The old bishop stirred restlessly as the wind howled in savage gusts against the castle and, although they had never met, he would have agreed with Corbett: Satan was abroad, his evil gathering like pus in an open wound.

FIVE

The next morning Corbett slept late, deaf to the sound of the abbey bells, and the normal bustle of the monks as they went about their various activities. He was awakened just before noon by the Master of Novices who announced that a message had come from John Benstede asking for Corbett to present himself at the castle immediately. Corbett hurriedly dressed, refused the kind offer of a horse but accepted the services of a guide to take him through Edinburgh to the castle. They set off through the drizzling rain, climbing the steep path up the rock which the monks said was popularly known as Arthur's Seat. Edinburgh was totally different from London; a royal burgh, it was built according to some sort of plan: long narrow streets with timbered and stone houses on either side, some joined together, others separated by narrow runnels or alleyways which led to a small garden or croft behind each tenement. There were shops, simple open-fronted affairs, booths and numerous ale-houses. Corbett thought London was dirty but Edinburgh was filthy; rubbish, the remains of meals, broken chamber-pots, even corpses of dead animals littered the streets.

The noise was intense with carts trundling across the rutted tracks or wynds as Corbett's guide described them. Business was brisk, shopkeepers even running out to grab

Corbett by the arm and offer a pie, a piece of cloth, fresh fish from the Firth, almonds, nuts and raisins brought in from the nearby port of Leith. Corbett could hardly understand their accent and was thankful for the stout staff his guide carried and so expertly used to make their way through the milling crowd. They passed the ancient church of St. Giles, and crossed a wide open grassy space which the guide called the Lawnmarket, the vast expanse generally used for markets or fairs. It was also the execution ground and the decomposing bodies of four criminals twirled from the makeshift gibbet.

They continued on, up the steep incline and into the castle. Inside, the scene was one of frenetic confusion, servants scurrying around, shouting and gesticulating, carts laden with provisions struggling to either get in or leave. Horses rearing and neighing, as ostlers and stable-boys tried to calm them down and lead them away. Men-at-arms, wearing the royal livery of Scotland, attempted to impose some form of order but the situation was not improved by a horde of courtiers standing around also issuing their instructions to a vast army of retainers all wearing different liveries. Corbett turned to his guide to ask what was happening but found the man had had enough sense and discretion to depart as quickly as possible. Corbett grabbed a groom who was trying to lead a horse to the stables at the far end of the bailey but the fool could not understand him and Corbett simply drew a blank look, followed by a shrug and muttered curses.

The English clerk stood rooted to the ground, wondering whether to stay or leave, when a hand gently touched his shoulder and he turned to see John Benstede, his kind face wrinkled in an apologetic smile. 'Master Clerk,' he said quietly. 'It was good of you to arrive so promptly. Come, let us leave this chaos.' Corbett followed him across the yard as the English envoy made his way carefully through the throng and up a flight of steep stairs into the main keep of the castle. Up another row of stairs and Corbett followed Benstede into a small, grim chamber with a bed of straw in the corner, a trestle table, a badly-lit brazier and a few rough stools for comfort. Benstede sighed and gestured to Corbett to sit down while he slumped, head on hand, on a stool near the table. 'What is the matter?' Corbett asked. 'Why the summons and why the confusion?' 'The Council of Guardians,' Benstede replied wearily, 'has called a meeting of the Great Council. We are not summoned to that but to the great banquet afterwards. The Chancellor, Bishop Wishart of Glasgow, has instructed all foreign envoys to attend this feast.' He poured a cup of watered wine for Corbett and then joined him, sipping carefully while studying the English clerk. 'You have been busy, Master Corbett?' he enquired. 'Yes,' Corbett replied tactfully. 'I have been trying to elicit what is happening in Scotland. Both our King and the Chancellor,' he lied, 'will be grateful for any information.' 'And have you discovered anything?' 'No,' Corbett lied again. 'Alexander III is dead, killed when his horse went over Kinghorn Ness. I have presented the Chancellor's condolences to his widow and now I must stay until I receive fresh instructions.' 'You are interested in Alexander III's death?' Benstede persisted. 'Do you think there was foul play?' 'I think,' Corbett replied carefully, 'that the King's death was mysterious and worthy of study.' Benstede pursed his lips and let out a long sigh. 'Be careful, Master Clerk,' he said. 'The Scots are in no mood to have foreigners, or Sassenachs as they call us, interfering in their affairs, but by all means keep yourself conversant with what is happening. Our Sovereign Lord King,' he commented sardonically, 'is always ready to listen to gossip from foreign courts.' Corbett decided to ignore the sarcastic tone and refused to be drawn. He stared at his companion's round cherubic face and twinkling blue eyes and knew that Benstede was only trying to draw him into conversation. 'What is the council meeting about?' he asked. Benstede got up and crossed to the bed in the far corner. He lifted the straw mattress and pulled out a small leather pouch which Corbett recognised as being in common use by clerks in the Chancery or envoys on their travels. Benstede inspected and then broke the seal and handed a small roll of vellum to Corbett. 'Read this,' he said. 'A draft copy of my report to the King. It describes the situation in Scotland as I see it and contains nothing confidential!' He grinned sideways at Corbett. 'At least, nothing yet! Go ahead! Read it!' Corbett unrolled the letter and ignored the usual introductory courtesies – "John Benstede to his Grace, etc. etc. The news from the Scottish court is this. His Grace, King Alexander III, was killed when he plunged from Kinghorn Ness on the night of the 18th March. It is commonly rumoured that the King was on his way to stay with his new wife, Queen Yolande, at a nearby manor. A great grief has fallen upon the kingdom and there is deep apprehension for the future. As your Grace knows, Alexander was married to your Grace's late lamented sister, Margaret. The issue of that marriage, the Princes Alexander and David, are dead. The only surviving issue is a granddaughter, Margaret, commonly called the Maid of Norway, offspring of Eric II of Norway, who married Alexander III's only surviving daughter. Margaret is a girl of only three years and is not of suitable age to take over this kingdom. Nevertheless, at Scone on the 5th February 1284, Alexander made all the estates of Scotland bind themselves by oath to acknowledge the Maid of Norway as his heir, failing any children Alexander might have in the future. Envoys have already been sent to the Norwegian court to apprise King Eric of the circumstances and to beg him to send the Maid back to Scotland as soon as possible.

"The situation, however, is still perilous. No woman has ever before become the ruler of Scotland and there are mutterings about the old Celtic tradition that when a king died the closest male relative took over the reins of power. This is now happening in Scotland and the kingdom is beginning to veer to one or the other of the two powerful families with such claims to the throne. These are the Comyns and the Bruces who can both reckon amongst their members males of the royal blood, for each claim the throne by descent from David, Earl of Huntingdon, great-uncle of Alexander III and grandson of a former king. There has always been bad blood between these families but now they are like two stiff-legged hunting-hounds who circle each other with hackles raised and teeth bared, carefully eyeing each other, ready to launch into war if any move is made by their rival. The only force which separates them is the Church, the one single coherent organisation in this country which binds like mortar the different races and degrees of this nation. Two of the leading churchmen, Bishops Wishart of Glasgow and Fraser of St. Andrews, have once more summoned to Scone the Prelates, Abbots, Priors, Earls, Barons and all good men of the country to renew their fealty to the new queen over the water, the Maid of Norway. All swore, on pain of excommunication and eternal damnation, to protect and uphold the peace of the land. Their Lordships, the Bishops, have achieved their ends, setting up a regency to represent the whole Community of the Realm consisting of the Earls of Buchan and Fife, Sir James Stewart and John Comyn and, of course, the two

Bishops themselves. Three of these so called Guardians are responsible for Scotland north of the Forth and the other three, particularly Wishart, wield authority south of this line. Men accept things as they are, though they would prefer things as they should be. Despite the Council of Guardians the different lords are levying troops and fortifying castles, preparing for war if peace fails. Your Grace, the King, has personal knowledge of the Bruces. All three of them, grandfather, father and son, all called Robert, never fail to remind people that they have royal blood in their veins and a strong claim to the Scottish throne. In 1238, as your Grace may know, when there was no apparent successor to the throne the then Scottish king called his magnates together and, in their presence and with their consent, designated the House of Bruce as his heir-presumptive. This promise proved illusory when a proper heir appeared. Nonetheless, the House of Bruce, for a brief while, tasted royalty and many claim it only whetted their appetite.

"As matters stand now, the kingdom is quiet, but I will keep your Grace informed of what events occur. We are acceptable to the Scottish court, being friends of all and allies to none. We are pleased to greet the arrival of Hugh Corbett, Clerk to the Chancery, despatched north by your Chancellor. His presence at the court will be a definite aid to our mission. God save your grace. Written at Edinburgh – May 1286."

Corbett studied the document and passed it back to Benstede. 'A fair analysis,' he commented, 'on the situation of Scotland. Do you think there will be war?' Benstede shook his head. 'No, not yet. Alexander kept his kingdom strong. It would take months, perhaps a year, for such strength to seep away. A great deal depends upon the arrival of the Maid from Norway and who secures her hand in marriage. When,' he nodded slowly, 'there could be war.' Their conversation then drifted on to other desultory matters. Corbett spoke about his early life, his wars in Wales and work at the Chancery. Benstede, the only son of a worthy Sussex farmer, told of his vocation to the priesthood, his interest in medicine and his rapid promotion in the royal service. Corbett caught the reference to medicine. 'You mean?' he asked, 'that you trained in the College of Medicine?' 'Yes,' Benstede replied. 'At one time I thought my vocation was to be a surgeon or doctor. I studied for a time in Paris, Padua and Salerno.' Benstede looked intently at Corbett. 'That is why I asked earlier if you were interested in the death of King Alexander. I myself questioned the royal physician who dressed the body for burial at Jedburgh Abbey, Duncan MacAirth. It was he who told me about the injuries the King received. He is here in the castle. Perhaps I can introduce him to you.' 'Does he keep some secret about the King's death?' Corbett asked. Benstede paused. 'No,' he replied. 'Alexander died from a broken neck due to a fall from his horse. Never mind the stupid prophecies and their curses! Alexander's first wife died, his two sons died; the way he drank to forget it all and his mad rides at night to satisfy any lust, it was only a matter of time before such an accident occurred.' 'So, Alexander's death came as no surprise to his subjects?' 'What do you mean?' Benstede replied sharply. 'I mean,' Corbett began slowly, 'the House of Comyn and that of Bruce must, er –,' the English clerk paused, searching for the right words. 'must not be displeased,' he continued, 'to be provided with an occasion to advance their respective claims to the Scottish throne.' 'Be careful what you say, Corbett!' Benstede replied. 'The Comyns hardly came to court and though Bruce was close to Alexander, the late King never bothered to consider their claims to his throne. Yet,' he concluded slowly, 'there are those who now watch Bruce carefully. He wants the crown, Master Corbett, as any other man wants eternal life. But, be careful in what you say or do. The Bruces are violent and would not take kindly to what you are hinting!' Corbett was nodding in agreement when a knock at the door interrupted them and a short, dumpy figure entered. Corbett was immediately repelled. The man had a bland, vacuous face, protruding green eyes and lank, brown, greasy hair. He made signs with his hands and fingers and Corbett watched fascinated as Benstede replied using identical gestures. The man looked at Corbett and Benstede turned. 'My apologies, Master Clerk. May I introduce Aaron, a convert from another faith, a deaf mute, who can only communicate in sign language. He is my body-servant, since my student days in Italy. He has come to tell us that the feast is about to begin and we must go down immediately.' Corbett nodded and followed both the envoy and his strange companion out of the room and down to the main hall of the castle.

SIX

The banquet was really a frantic blur to Corbett. The long hall was caparisoned with cloths of Paris, costly arras, and ablaze with torches burning fiercely in their countless sconces along the walls. At the far end, on a dais, was a long table crowded with fierce-looking men dressed in costly ermine and sable-edged cloaks, though, from where he stood, Corbett could see the glint of armour many of them wore beneath their robes. Even so, the Council of Guardians were intent on keeping the peace; weapons were forbidden and royal serjeants-at-arms were placed in groups in the shadowy recesses of the hall. Beneath the great silver-encrusted salt bowl were long rows of tables crowded with the retainers, clerks and officials of the great lords. The noise was intense, constant chatter, voices raised in argument, an air of expectancy, even tension, as everyone pretended to be involved in what was happening around them but secretly watched the great ones at the high table.

Benstede swept through the hall and tactfully presented himself before this array of the most powerful magnates in Scotland. He also introduced Corbett who felt many of the lords were too busy to acknowledge him though he noticed Bishop Wishart of Glasgow, a wizened little man with a face as brown and as wrinkled as a shrivelled walnut, studying him intently beneath heavy-lidded eyes. There was another, a giant with steel-grey hair, piercing blue eyes and a cruel mouth. Benstede later named him as Lord Robert, the leader of the Bruce faction. He too studied Corbett intently before reverting to stare fiercely down the hall.

Benstede and Corbett then sat at the edge of a table directly beneath the great dais just as a chorus of trumpets brayed. Bishop Wishart mumbled grace and the feasting began. A group of musicians with flute, rebec and drum attempted to make music but they were easily drowned by the roar of conversation as the courses were served. Corbett had heard that the Scots were a crude race but their cooks could have held their own with the best in Europe. Each guest had a trencher or plate of hard stale bread which served as a dish for a series of rich foods served by harassed, sweating boys who had to feed countless mouths and, at the same time, avoid the secretly lecherous hands of certain of the guests. There was brawn, a meat boiled with sugar and cloves, thickened with cinnamon and ginger and garnished with boar ribs. Fresh pork embellished with egg-yolk, pine cones, raisins, saffron and pepper and baked in pastry; fish tarts; roasted lampreys; mutton, plover, curlew, snipe and pheasant. Wine was splashed from jug to cup and then often drained in one loud gulp. Corbett ate sparingly as he always did. The sight of one of the boys rubbing a festering ear, while carrying food, also diminished his appetite. He sipped gently at the wine, exchanging pleasantries with Benstede, who led the conversation into the intricacies of Scottish policies. 'Look around, Corbett; this hall is full of men who would love to cut each other's throats. Alexander held them fast in a strong mailed fist. God knows what will happen now! 'What do you think?' Corbett asked. 'It's what

I dread,' Benstede replied. 'Under the wrong king this tide of violence might swirl and sweep south across the border.' Corbett quietly agreed, remembering the deserted countryside he had passed through on his way to Scotland. Wide expanses of undefended countryside vulnerable to sudden attack for pillage or even conquest. Benstede leaned across the table to talk further but, aware of the growing interest of neighbours, stared knowingly at Corbett and lapsed into silence. The conversation ebbed and swirled about them. Corbett could scarcely understand some of the accents and contented himself with gazing around. Another group of men across the aisle on the opposite table were equally detached, and one of them was staring at Benstede's back with such venom that Corbett became alarmed. He leaned over the table and grasped Benstede's arm. 'The group behind you!' he whispered. 'The group behind me,' Benstede dourly interrupted, 'are French envoys with their leader, Armand de Craon. A small, dark, intense man with a beard and drooping moustache, who is probably looking at me as if he would like to put daggers in my back?' Corbett nodded. 'Good!' Benstede smiled. 'I sat deliberately with my back to him. De Craon can never resist an insult.' 'Why is he here?' Corbett asked. 'The same as us,' Benstede retorted. 'To watch the situation and report back to that stone-faced hypocritical bastard, Philip IV of France. Of course, there are other reasons.' Benstede looked round and leaned conspiratorially across the table. 'De Craon must be wondering what we are discussing. His master, Philip IV of France, would dearly love two things now Scotland has lost a strong king. First, to seek an alliance with the Scots and so divert our Liege Lord's justifiable pursuit of his claims over English lands in France. Secondly,' Benstede ran his finger round the rim of his wine cup. 'Secondly,

Philip hopes Edward will lay claim to Scotland and so become immersed in a tangled and lengthy war.' 'And will he?' Corbett asked innocently. Benstede grimaced. 'No!' he replied. 'Edward of England will only eat what he can digest!'

Corbett nodded and was going to pursue the matter further when suddenly a commotion at the far end of the table drew all eyes and silenced the clamour in the hall. Two young men, their sallow faces flushed with wine, were standing, knives in hand, each waiting for the other to lunge or parry. Corbett thought it was mere drunken bravado when one of them lunged across the table and uproar ensued as food, cups and flagons of wine and ale were sent sprawling. Guests rose from their seats, men pushing and shoving each other. Knives were drawn and it looked as if many ancient, long-held grudges were to be settled. Corbett pushed through the crowd to get away and stood with his back to a pillar. He never really understood what happened next except it was one of those chances, the movement of fortune's wheel, or the sudden intervention of God's saving grace. But a trumpet brayed out and Corbett, turning to look, felt the dagger whip by his cheek and clash against the pillar. The clerk, startled, looked round, but could see no obvious assailant in the milling crowd around him. He stooped and picked up the cruel dagger which had nearly split his throat. It was possibly one of hundreds carried and used in this hall for eating. Corbett let it drop as the trumpets brayed again and royal serjeants-at-arms, staves in their hands, moved into the hall and began to impose order. Tables and benches were put right, the unconscious bodies revived and the two young men who had started the fray were led bloodied and dishevelled from the hall.

The banquet recommenced but the fray had dampened

and soured the atmosphere. Corbett took his seat, trying to ignore de Craon who was grinning as if he had suddenly found something amusing. Benstede, who returned looking untidy with streaks of dirt on his face, muttered that he had been manhandled, probably by the French, and was intent on leaving as soon as possible. Other guests now rose to leave and the two English envoys got up and began to move amongst the different groups. Aaron, Benstede's body-servant, appeared as if from nowhere and both he and his master moved away as Corbett turned to see the French leave, de Craon still smirking. Benstede had told Corbett he need not return to the Abbey but could bed down in the hall with the other retainers and he gratefully accepted the offer. He felt tired, slightly drunk and frightened; if an assassin was hunting him then the dark runnels of Edinburgh at night would only provide fresh opportunities. Corbett was looking for a suitable place as the crowd began to disperse when Benstede returned, accompanied by a thin, stooping figure with watery eyes, a drinker's red nose and a wispy beard. The newcomer was ostentatiously dressed in robes slashed with yellow taffeta and bound by a gold cord very similar to one used by Benstede, although the latter had a row of knots in his to prevent it slipping down over the loops on his gown. 'Master Corbett,' Benstede said. 'May I introduce the great master of medicine and royal physician, Duncan MacAirth.' Corbett looked at the old drunken face and knew Benstede was being sardonic. MacAirth would be a charlatan like many of his kind, concealing his ignorance behind an arrogant poise, strange concoctions, astrology and horoscopes. Yet he bowed in respect; Benstede left with a wink and a perfunctory nod, telling Corbett he hoped to see him again.

Corbett led MacAirth to the nearest table, cleared a

space and gestured to him to sit. 'Master MacAirth,' he said, pouring two cups of wine. 'I am grateful for your attention in this matter. I understand you dressed the late King's body for burial. I wondered ...' 'No wonder, Corbett,' MacAirth almost screeched in reply, seizing the proffered cup and slurping noisily from it. 'No wonder. The King was found by a patrol of mounted serjeants sent out by the guid Bishop Wishart. He was found on the rocks beneath Kinghorn Ness; his horse, his favourite white mare called Tamesin was near by. Both horse and rider had their necks broken. The King's corpse, together with the saddle and bridle, was brought back here to the castle.' 'Were there other injuries?' Corbett enquired. 'Of course,' MacAirth retorted, blowing stale wine fumes into Corbett's face. 'The King's legs were broken, there were injuries from head to toe. You must realise that the King not only fell from a great height but the sea pounded his body to and fro against the rocks.' He lowered his voice. 'The face was a mass of shredded flesh. Almost unrecognisable.' 'You are sure it was the King?' MacAirth stared back, a strange look in his drink-sodden face. 'Aye, it was the King.' He laughed, a sharp neighing sound. 'Mind you, Alexander would have liked that. He loved disguises and masques.' He sighed. 'But this game has gone on too long. No, Corbett, Alexander died from a fall from a cliff. His corpse was boiled, the flesh separated from the bones, stuffed with spices and sealed in a lead coffin and taken to Jedburgh Abbey to be amongst his ancestors.' 'When was the funeral?' Corbett snapped. MacAirth squinted down at the wine-stained table and muttered to himself. 'The King died on the 18th March and the burial took place eleven days later on the 29th March.' 'Was not that rather hasty?' Corbett asked. MacAirth grimaced and drew shapes on the table with the spilled wine. 'No,' he replied. 'The King was not a pretty sight. The sea had soaked his corpse; even with the spices, it was hard to keep him presentable.' 'Did the Queen come to inspect the corpse?' 'No,' the reply was curt. 'She has never moved from Kinghorn. Why,' he asked, trying to focus his bleary eyes on Corbett, 'Why do you ask all these questions?' 'Curiosity,' Corbett replied soothingly. 'Simple curiosity, Master MacAirth. But tell me, Master Physician, for I see you are an astute man, what happened to the two squires, the valets of the chamber, who accompanied the King?' 'It's strange you mention that,' MacAirth muttered. 'Patrick Seton evidently rode too far ahead of the King and actually reached Kinghorn. When the King was found dead he returned here to the castle and closeted himself in his room.' MacAirth heaved a sigh. 'He was questioned and visited by everyone, including Master Benstede, the French envoy, Bruce, Comyn, Wishart, but he seemed witless. Even I could do nothing. He simply sat muttering to himself.' 'What?' Corbett asked. 'Nothing of importance, he just mumbled about shadows, shadows on the Kinghorn Ness. Can you make sense of that?' 'No,' Corbett replied. 'But the second squire? What of him?' MacAirth yawned and rose. 'I must retire,' he snapped. 'Your questions exhaust me. The second squire, Thomas Erceldoun, is still here. He, too, has been questioned but he is not the most intelligent of men, or the best of horse-riders. His mount threw him and he stayed on the beach, witnesses swear to that. I am afraid he's the laughing-stock of the court, despised by most and pitied by the few who listen to his constant pleas of innocence. I must away. I will send Erceldoun to you tomorrow. You are staying at the castle tonight?' Corbett nodded. 'Yes, here in the hall,' he replied. 'I do thank you for your courtesy, Master MacAirth.' The physician nodded and curtly bade Corbett farewell. The clerk rose, stretched and looked around the deserted hall now darkening as the torches spluttered out. He chose a place between two snoring servants and laid down to sleep, oblivious to the figure watching him from the shadows.

The silent watcher stared through the darkness at the place where Corbett had settled down to sleep. He would have liked to have driven his dagger straight into the interfering clerk's throat but knew this was not the time nor the occasion. He bitterly regretted that the knife thrown during the banquet had not hit its target for he had recognised Corbett as a dangerous man. Quiet, unobtrusive, but always asking questions, gathering information, Corbett must have learnt something from that fool MacAirth. Under his breath the man quietly cursed the interfering clerk who could bring his master's grand design to nothing. Nevertheless, there would be other times, other places. Scotland was a desolate country with deserted roads and lonely heaths. One day he would find Corbett exposed and vulnerable and deal with him in his own sophisticated way.

SEVEN

The next morning Corbett was shaken awake. He turned, stiff and cold, to see an anxious young man, blond cropped hair, worried eyes and pock-marked face. 'Master Corbett,' he urged. 'Master Corbett, wake up!' Corbett struggled to his feet and stared around the hall where the rest of the sleepers there were slowly rising to their feet, some nursing sore heads, others bawling for wine and food. He turned to the young man who had woken him. 'In God's teeth!' he snapped. 'Who are you?' 'Thomas Erceldoun,' the young man replied. 'Master MacAirth said that you wished to talk to me.' He gestured to the nearest table. 'I have brought you some ale and rye bread.' Corbett nodded his thanks, rubbed the back of his neck to ease the stiffness, and sat down. 'You were with the late King on the night he died?' Erceldoun swallowed nervously. 'Aye,' he replied. 'I was with the King. I've told my story many times.' The young man paused to gather his breath and Corbett, still only half awake, felt pity for this young man whose life and energy were now narrowed to justify his conduct on one night out of thousands. Corbett rubbed his eyes wearily, yawned and then saw the hurt in Erceldoun's eyes. 'I am sorry for disturbing you,' Erceldoun blurted out. 'But the physician who works in the royal household said that you wanted to see me immediately. I was afraid I might miss you. I ...' 'Nonsense,' Corbett interrupted kindly. 'There is no need for excuses.' He sipped the cup of the cold watered ale. 'Please tell me what happened on that wild, tragic night?'

Erceldoun immediately rushed into his story, how the King decided at the banquet to return to Kinghorn and summoned both Seton and himself to ride with him. Both had remonstrated with the King when he withdrew to his private chambers in the castle to dress for the journey. 'He was very excited,' Erceldoun explained. 'He said he must leave that night and taunted us as cowards. So we went. We rode north to the ferry and, God knows how, got across the Forth. The royal purveyor was waiting with fresh mounts; the King's white horse, Tamesin, was already saddled, and his Grace left immediately with Seton. I had, as you know, trouble with my horse as soon as I left the beach!' Corbett thought of the drunken purveyor. 'Did the purveyor also attempt to restrain the King?' he asked. Erceldoun nodded. 'Yes, but the King would have none of it.' 'Did the King check his saddle and girth straps?' 'No,' Erceldoun replied. 'The King and Seton left immediately. My horse was skittish, I could not settle him. Why?' he asked hopefully. 'Do you think that Tamesin was not properly saddled?' 'Perhaps,' Corbett lied for he knew that if it was not, the accident could well have occurred earlier. 'And Seton?' Corbett continued. 'What happened to him?' 'He arrived at Kinghorn,' Erceldoun wearily replied. 'Then came back here late the following day after the King's death became public. He just withdrew to his room; the more he was questioned the more witless he seemed, muttering about shadows on Kinghorn Ness.' 'He was devoted to the King?' Erceldoun looked sharply at Corbett. 'Of course,' he almost snapped. 'As was I. But others say different,' he added bitterly. 'They allege that we deserted the King because we were afraid. They forget about our journey across the Firth!' 'How did Seton die?' 'I do not know,' Erceldoun answered. 'Perhaps of a broken heart. He ate little and would not speak. He was found dead in his chamber and was given a hasty funeral.' 'There was no mark of violence on his body?' Corbett cautiously asked. Erceldoun narrowed his eyes. 'I, too, thought of that but, no, I inspected the corpse.' 'Then perhaps poison was administered?' 'No,' Erceldoun emphatically replied. 'He ate little and it was I who brought him food. Visitors sent or brought him small gifts.' 'Who?' Corbett asked. 'Members of the Council. Especially after Bishop Wishart visited him and announced that Seton was not guilty of any involvement in the King's death.' 'So there was suspicion?' Corbett enquired. Erceldoun swallowed and looked round nervously. 'King Alexander,' he whispered nervously, 'was a man of strong appetites. Seton was a valet of his chamber. There were rumours that, that ...' 'That the King used Seton?' Corbett interjected. Erceldoun nodded. 'The King had been a widower for ten years,' he continued. 'Seton was jealous and hurt at the King's passion for Queen Yolande. But he would never have harmed the King. Anyway,' he concluded morosely, 'it was established that he arrived in Kinghorn at the expected time.' 'So, despite the King riding a better horse, Seton was in front?' Corbett asked. 'Of course. Seton knew the terrain better. I suspect the King found it difficult and, for a while, lost his way in the dark. Seton would have gone ahead believing the King would not be far behind. We always travelled like that; Seton's task was to ensure that there were no obstacles.' Erceldoun paused. 'It was my task to follow at the rear!' 'Such things do happen,' Corbett soothingly replied. 'But tell me. Who else visited Seton?' 'Everyone,' Erceldoun muttered. 'Bishop Wishart, the Lord Bruce, members of the court. The French envoy and, of course, Master Benstede. He sent Seton a bowl of almonds and raisins and a present of velvet gloves.' 'Did Seton eat the food?' 'A little,' Erceldoun said. 'As with everything, I ate the rest.' 'Then why the presents?' 'Oh,' Erceldoun bitterly commented, 'before the King's death, Seton was a popular man. Anyone who wished to see the King would often approach Seton. Benstede was not the only one to send gifts.' Erceldoun looked round at the servants who were now busy, slowly clearing the cold, congealed messes left by the previous night's banquet. Officers and marshals of the royal household were shouting orders. Dogs, noisily barking, wandered in from the courtyard and were busy sniffing amongst the rubbish. Erceldoun rose and looked down at Corbett. 'I must go,' he said. 'There are duties to be carried out.' He nodded at Corbett and walked out of the hall.

The English clerk watched him go and realised that he, too, must return to the abbey. There was so much he had learnt, so many facts, so many happenings. His legs and back ached, he needed the quiet, clean, pure atmosphere of the monastery to settle his mind and probe all he had learnt. He gathered his cloak and entered the bailey, a calmer place than the previous day. He drew water from the well, splashed his hands and face and left the castle, a lonely, weary figure totally ignored by every one. Outside he stopped and realised that he would have to make his own way back. He remembered the dagger thrown during the banquet and decided it would be safer to return through the crowded town than venture into the marshy wooded countryside. He knew the way vaguely from the journey the night before and the careful directions given to him by the Prior.

Corbett trudged down the beaten, muddy track; the sky

was overcast and a light rain began to fall. A passing cart rolled by splattering him with mud and Corbett quietly cursed Burnell for sending him here. He reached the town and entered the Lawnmarket; there was a crowd gathered watching some wretch being dragged by horses across the open space to a waiting scaffold. The man, bound hand and foot, was pinioned to a sheet of hard-boiled leather, which the two horses pulled across the mud: the man screamed as the hard ground battered his naked back, while he had to endure the taunts and filth hurled by the onlookers, the strictures of the city officials and the droning monotony of the praying priest. Corbett did not stay but pushed through the throng of people and walked on. He kept to the centre of the street away from the rubbish which littered the entrances and walks of the miserable timbered houses. The shops and stalls were open for business: a cart bearing a ragged, crudely-drawn banner was used as a stage by a troupe of actors shouting words that Corbett could not understand. Shopkeepers bawled and yelled at him. "Hot sheeps' feet!" "Ribs of beef!" Greasy hands clawed at his arms but he pushed them off. The smell of fresh bread from a bakery made him hungry but he did not stop.

Corbett was tired, depressed: the passing sights caught his eye: a dog, one leg shorter than the rest, sniffing at the bloated body of a rat: a cat running by, his mouth stuffed with baby mice, a beggar, white-eyed and sore-ridden, shrieking at young boys who were pissing over him. Corbett remembered the teachings of Augustine, "Sin is the breakdown of all relationships". If that was so, Corbett thought, then sin was all around him. Here in these dirty streets, a lonely English clerk: his wife and child dead, years gone: the only woman he had ever loved since, a convicted murderer and traitor, consumed by fire at

Smithfield in London. Now, here alone amidst strangers who sought his death. He thought of Ranulf, his body-servant, and wished he was here, not sick with the fever, miles away in some English monastery.

He passed the church of St. Giles, turned into another winding street and almost walked into the two figures standing there. Corbett muttered an apology and stepped to one side. One of the men moved to block his path. 'Comme ça va, Monsieur?' 'Qu'est ce que ce?' Corbett spontaneously replied, then repeated, 'What is the matter? I don't speak French. Get out of my way!' 'No, Monsieur,' the man replied in perfect English. 'You are in our way. Come! We wish to talk to you.' 'Go and be hanged!' Corbett muttered and tried to go on. 'Monsieur. There are two of us and two more behind you. We mean you no harm.' The Frenchman turned and beckoned with his hand. 'Come, Monsieur. We will not keep you. We will not harm you. Come!' Corbett looked at the two well-fed, thick-set men, and, hearing a slight sound behind him, knew there were more. 'I come,' he grimaced. The men led him down an alleyway, stinking from dog urine and heaps of excrement. They stopped outside a small house, single-storeyed, one window beneath its dripping, soggy thatch roof, and a battered ale-stake jutting out from beneath the eaves.

There was one dank, damp room inside with an earth-beaten floor, two small trestle tables and a collection of rough stools fashioned out of old barrels. It was deserted except for a group sitting round one table being served ale by the frightened proprietor. A slattern, evidently his wife, looked on fearfully. A group of children, their dirty faces streaked with tears, clung to her tattered gown and stared round-eyed at the group of men who had commandeered the room and were now talking quickly in an alien language. Corbett immediately recognised de Craon, who rose as he entered, gave a half-mocking bow and waved him to a stool. 'It was good of you to come, Master Clerk,' he said in perfect English with only a trace of a French accent. 'I understand that you have been very busy in Edinburgh asking many questions, poking your nose into matters that do not concern you. Here,' he pushed a cup of ale towards Corbett. 'Come. Drink this. Tell us about the real reason you are here.' 'Why don't you ask Benstede?' Corbett retorted. 'You have no right to detain me here. Neither the English nor the Scottish courts will be happy to hear that French envoys are detaining people at their whim!' De Craon shrugged, his hands extended in an expansive gesture. 'But, Monsieur Corbett, we are not detaining you. We have asked you here and you have accepted our invitation. You are free to come and go as you wish. But,' he continued smoothly, 'now that you are here, I know you are too curious to let the matter drop.' He sat back on his stool, his brown, beringed hands gently folded in his lap, staring at Corbett like some understanding elder brother or patronising uncle. Corbett moved the cup of ale back across the table. 'No, you tell me, Monsier de Craon, why you are here and why you wish to speak to me?' 'We are here,' de Craon began smoothly, 'to represent our master's interests and to establish a better relationship between King Philip IV and the Scottish throne. We were achieving considerable successes right up to the moment of the late King's sudden and unfortunate death in which you show a great deal of interest.' 'Yes, it does interest me,' Corbett replied tersely. 'I am a good clerk. I am here at the request of the English court and they, like Philip IV, are interested in any information we can send.' De Craon shook his head slowly in disbelief. 'All of that,' he replied, 'could be done by Benstede, so why are you here?' He wagged an admonitory finger to fend off any protest from Corbett. 'I believe that you are not really interested in Alexander III's fall from a cliff. There are other secret reasons. Perhaps an alliance with the Bruces or the Comyns? Perhaps you even bear a secret claim by King Edward himself to be ruler of Scotland!'

Corbett stared at de Craon in amazement. He suddenly realised that the French really did believe that he was here on a secret and delicate diplomatic mission on Edward I's behalf, that his interest in Alexander III's death was mere drapery, a trick to conceal his true task. The ridiculousness of the situation made him smile and, throwing his head back, he burst into peals of laughter. De Craon started forward, his face flushed with anger, and Corbett drew back, believing that de Craon was on the point of striking him. 'I didn't know you found us so amusing!' Corbett composed himself. 'I don't,' he replied sternly, 'and I did not find the incident last night entertaining or acceptable!' The Frenchman simply shrugged and glanced away. 'Moreover,' Corbett added, 'you seem to have answered your own questions. Are you, Monsieur de Craon, here too to make a secret alliance to take advantage of a kingdom without a king?' 'What do you mean?' de Craon snapped back. 'I mean,' Corbett said forcefully, 'that for two decades Alexander III ruled this country with little or no assistance from the French. Now he is dead with no strong heir. Is it not possible that French influence can be made to be felt once more? 'And what about your master?' de Craon almost shouted. 'You know that Bruce is a friend of his! 'What do you mean?' Corbett innocently enquired. 'I mean that Bruce, like Edward, went on crusade and that Bruce gave Edward every assistance in his civil war against the now dead Simon de Montfort. He fought at Lewes on Edward's behalf and at other battles. Bruce has a claim to the Scottish throne. Why should Edward now object to his old friend and comrade-in-arms seizing the Scottish crown?' Corbett rose from his stool and sent it flying back with a crash. He sensed de Craon's comrades behind him, tense, expectant, ready to act. 'Why not?' he asked sardonically. 'Why don't you ask Benstede these questions? I am sure he will give you satisfactory answers.' Corbett then turned on his heel and strode out of the room and made his way back up the alley. He tensed himself, ears straining, wondering if the French would pursue him and, when he safely reached the top of the alleyway, breathed a sigh of relief and continued on his way back to the Abbey of Holy Rood.

Eventually Corbett was free of the town and into the stretch of countryside which surrounded the abbey. The rain was falling more heavily. He pulled his cloak more firmly round his body and threaded his way through the trees. He was still on his guard, fearful of any pursuit by de Craon or his men. The trees on either side were dark and quiet, the only sound being the rustling of branches and the soft pitter-patter of the rain on the leaves. Then he heard a noise. He thought it was a twig breaking but then something jolted his memory. Corbett had heard such a sound many times during his war in Wales and, without thinking, threw himself on his face. He heard the sound again, followed by the whistle and thud of a crossbow bolt whirring overhead to slam into the nearest tree. Corbett waited no longer. He knew that the archer would have to load and winch his bow, so he rose and ran with all his force, clearing the trees, almost breathless as he stumbled up the muddy causeway leading to the main abbey gate. He made the mistake of turning round, stumbled and fell on one knee and then rose, sobbing in terror as he clawed his way to the main gate, hammering on it with all his might. The door opened and he staggered, almost fell, into the arms of the astonished lay brother. Corbett quickly regained his composure, gave the monk a hasty lie, and hurriedly made his way to the Prior's quarters. The chamber was empty so Corbett went straight to his room, threw himself down upon his cot and fell into a deep and dreamless sleep.

EIGHT

For the second time that day, Corbett was shaken awake, an insistent voice calling his name. He opened his eyes and started as he recognised the white anxious face, staring green eyes and tousled hair of his servant, Ranulf, whom he had last seen in the infirmary of Tynemouth Priory. Corbett shook himself awake. 'Ranulf! When did you arrive?' 'About an hour ago,' Ranulf replied, 'with my horse and a pack mule. I remembered your instruction to join you at the Abbey of Holy Rood. I have spent most of the day just finding my way here from the castle.' He looked Corbett up and down. 'Where have you been? You're covered in mud!' 'A long story,' Corbett testily replied. 'I will tell you later. For the time being, find the Prior and tell him that I am back and arrange for some hot water to be brought here.' Ranulf swiftly departed. His master, he thought, was as strange as ever, close, careful, even secretive and still intent on cleanliness. He wondered what had brought Corbett north; he had tried to find out all the way to Tynemouth but Corbett remained taciturn, so Ranulf became sullen. He owed his life to Corbett who had saved him from a choking death at Tyburn, yet Corbett was still mysterious; working constantly, his only pleasure being the flute, some manuscript or sitting quietly over a cup of wine brooding about life. Ranulf had cursed his departure from London away from the young wife of a London mercer. He felt a tightness in his groin and muttered foul oaths: she was a fine lady with her laces and bows and arrogant looks but, between the sheets, a different matter, soft and pleading, turning and twisting beneath him. Ranulf sighed heavily, a long way from this dour monastery and his secretive master.

Corbett was, in fact, very pleased to see Ranulf again. He would not admit it but he felt secure with Ranulf who would guard his back. Corbett was completely mystified by his servant's energy and zest for life and passionate attachment to any woman who arched an eyebrow at him. But Ranulf was here and while Corbett bathed and changed his clothing, he wondered how Ranulf could protect him from the secret assassins now stalking him. The attack in the forest was attempted murder and he now drew the same conclusion about the dagger thrown at him the previous day.

Corbett spent the rest of the evening analysing what he knew and had learnt but soon realised that he had been drawn into a maze of marshy morass and the more he probed, the more puzzled he became. He did not talk to Ranulf about the problem but listened with half an ear to the young man's description of his stay at Tynemouth as he wondered what to do next. Corbett felt inclined to draw up a report for Burnell. This would at least enumerate the problems he now faced, and acquaint the Chancellor about his complete lack of progress. He finally decided against this. So far he had only spoken to minor figures of the tragedy which befell Alexander III at Kinghorn. Benstede and de Craon could give little information. Perhaps the great ones of the land knew something different and should be approached. Moreover, Corbett realised that if de Craon knew he was asking questions it was only a matter of time before the Council of Guardians intervened and either put a stop to his activities or expelled him from the country. He therefore had to work quickly and collect some information to take back to Burnell in London.

After Compline, the last service of the day, Corbett approached the Prior and asked him where he could meet Robert Bruce. The Prior, no man's fool, stared hard at Corbett and shook his head in warning. 'Be very careful, Master Clerk. I suspect what you are involved in. I have heard vague rumours, comments, court gossip. These are troubled times and you have decided to fish in very dangerous and deep waters.' Corbett shrugged. 'I have no choice,' he replied. 'Each of us has his tasks, I have mine. I do not know what you have heard and I will not ask. I do no man any harm and perhaps may achieve a great good. That is why I wish to see the Lord Bruce.' The Prior sighed. 'Normally the Bruces are in their mountain castle across the country on the River Clyde but, because of the late King's death, Bruce stays near Edinburgh. After all,' the Prior continued sardonically, 'he has no desire to see the cake taken while his back is turned. Rumour has it that he has taken up residence in the port of Leith, near enough to Edinburgh but, should matters go wrong, the best place for his departure by land or sea. Nevertheless, I will check to see if this is correct and inform you tomorrow.'

The next morning when the bells of the abbey tolled for Prime, the first prayer of the monastic day, Corbett was up, dressed and gently kicked a sleepy, grunting Ranulf awake. They joined the long silent line of monks filing into the church. Corbett sang the psalms with them, feeling a great deal of the tension within him dissipate with the monotonous, harmonious chant. Ranulf sat slumped in the bench beside him, groaning and muttering at his master.

After the service was over, they broke their fast in the small whitewashed refectory before approaching the Prior who confirmed his speculation of the previous evening that the Lord Bruce and his entourage had taken up residence in the port of Leith. Corbett and Ranulf immediately took their leave and were through the abbey gates travelling north to Leith just as the sun rose. They made fair progress. Corbett felt refreshed though still wary, pleased that the previous day's rainclouds had now disappeared and hoping that the Lord Bruce was still in Leith and would grant him an audience. They skirted the city, threading their way through the still-silent streets and, following the Prior's careful directions, soon found themselves on the broad beaten approach to the port of Leith. This was busy with carts and pack-horses making their way into Edinburgh, bringing in the products from both port and countryside to be sold at the markets. Wagon-loads of fish, fruit, salted meat, English wool and Flemish velvets, each wagon jostling for a place on the rutted track. The drivers, flushed and cursing, each trying to be the first into the city and to have their wares ready for sale before the city came to life.

Corbett rode quietly between them, keeping a wary eye on Ranulf who, after staring round-eyed at everything, began to mimic the strange accents, and drew dark looks from a number of passers-by. Corbett urged him to keep quiet and was more than relieved when they entered the narrow, winding, rutted streets of Leith and made their way to the small market square. Here Corbett began to question any respectable citizen on the whereabouts of the Lord Bruce's household and described to Ranulf the insignia of Bruce's retinue in the hope that his sharp-eyed servant might discover .someone wearing this livery. Neither seemed able to elicit any information. Many of the townsfolk could not understand them and Ranulf, particularly, found it difficult to cope with the broad flow of Scottish his questions provoked. They drew a small crowd of bystanders who, finding they were English, began to mutter and curse. Corbett realised that this was Leith, a Scottish port, whose ships were often in conflict with English vessels. He had forgotten this unofficial war and damned his own foolhardiness at not taking the matter into account.

At last they decided to withdraw from the square and were on the point of departure when they were suddenly surrounded by a group of tough-looking soldiers, helmeted and armed. Their leader grabbed the bridle of Corbett's horse and asked him a question he could not understand. The man repeated it, this time in atrocious French. Corbett nodded. Yes, he announced, he was an English clerk. He bore greetings from the Chancellor of England to the Lord Bruce and sought an audience with him. The man's wolfish face broke into a grin, displaying a set of decay-blackened teeth. 'Oh well,' he replied in French. 'If an English clerk wants to see the Lord Bruce, then that can be arranged.' He slipped a hand beneath Corbett's cloak and deftly drew out the clerk's knife which he stuck into his own sturdy leather-studded belt, and almost dragged the horse across the market-place. The rest of his party brought up the rear, baiting and goading Ranulf, who gave as good as he got with a stream of obscene English oaths. They left the market-place for a maze of streets and eventually came to a large stone two-storeyed house with a timbered roof, its exquisite carved eaves jutting out over a small courtyard beneath. Both Corbett and Ranulf were dragged unceremoniously off their horses and pushed through the main door of the house and down a passageway which led into the main room or hall.

Corbett realised it must be some wealthy merchant's dwelling which Bruce had either commandeered or rented. It was clean, there were carpets on the floor, a tapestry on the far end wall with spring green boughs around the room to give a pleasant odour. There was even a fireplace set in the wall and, seated at the head of a long polished table, was the Lord Bruce. He was eating a mess of pottage and taking deep gulps of wine from a large ornamental cup.

He did not bother to look up when Corbett and Ranulf were ushered in but made a gesture for them to sit on the bench alongside the table while he continued noisily with his meal. At last he finished, gave a loud belch and wiped his greasy fingers and mouth on the hem of his ermine-lined cloak. The guard who had brought them went up beside the chair, knelt and spoke quietly to Bruce in a language Corbett could not understand and guessed that it was probably Gaelic, a language totally alien to him. He felt afraid, for Bruce, despite having passed the biblical age of three score years and ten, had a reputation as a ferocious warrior. A man of vaulting ambitions with the talents to match, passionately devoted to his house and ambitious for his favourite grandson, the twelve-year-old Robert, making no secret now that Alexander III was dead that the House of Bruce had the best claim to the Scottish throne. His appearance only enhanced his reputation, a leonine head, steel-grey hair, sharp, shrewd eyes. A cruel predatory face. No fool. A man who did not care about the consequences of his actions.

The soldier eventually stopped talking. Bruce nodded and gestured at him to withdraw and turned to Corbett. 'So, Master English Clerk,' he spoke slowly. 'You wish to see me? Why?' Bruce peered closer. 'I saw you the other evening,' he said. 'At the banquet in the castle. You were with that cold-eyed English envoy, Benstede, were you not?' Corbett nodded and opened his mouth to speak but Bruce brushed him aside with a peremptory wave of his hand. 'I do not like people coming to see me unannounced,' he explained. 'I am not some petty chieftain with time on his hands to exchange chatter and gossip. Moreover, I don't trust English clerks who go around asking questions as if Scotland was another English shire. So I will ask you once again, Master Clerk, what are you doing here?' 'My Lord,' Corbett began nervously, 'may I present the compliments and affectionate greetings of my master, Robert Burnell, Chancellor of England and Bishop of Bath and Wells.' 'Nonsense,' Bruce barked in reply. 'I knew Burnell when I was in England. I did not like him then and he did not like me. The passing of the years has done little to improve the situation. So, Master Clerk, what now?'

Corbett smiled. 'I see I cannot bluff you, my Lord. The truth is that I was sent to Scotland to find out what happened, is happening and might happen.' He looked hard at Bruce, summoning up enough false honesty to cover his lies. 'You must realise that, my Lord. You have served with King Edward, you know his mind.' 'Yes,' Bruce replied. 'I know his crafty mind. He is a lion in war but a panther in fickleness and inconstancy, changing his word and promise, cloaking himself in pleasant speech. When cornered he promises whatever you wish but, as soon as he escapes, he forgets his promise. The treachery and falsehood he uses to advance his cause he calls prudence, and the path by which he attains his ends, however crooked, he calls straight, whatever he says is lawful.' Bruce stopped, his chest heaving angrily, to wipe the spittle from his mouth. Corbett just sat quiet. Bruce glared at him. 'Have you ever heard this, Master Clerk?' and he immediately launched into poetry, quoting an old Scottish prophecy about England:

Edward of England has leopards three
Let Scots keep all in sight,
While two in front, their smile you see,
The one to the rear can fight.

Corbett smiled wanly. Bruce was now in a foul temper and very dangerous. 'I am sure the verse has some truth in it, my Lord,' he replied. 'But what can I say? Alexander III of Scotland has left us as an heir a three-year-old Norwegian princess. In England,' Corbett hurried on, 'we are still confused about the late King's death.' 'Nonsense,' Bruce replied. 'The late King was notorious for his mad rides at dusk to tumble any girl above the age of twelve.' 'In England, sir,' Corbett replied tartly, 'they say he was drunk, but you were at the Council that evening. As you are the leading peer of the realm, surely you know the truth!' 'Aye, I was there!' Bruce answered. 'The King was not drunk.' 'Perhaps the King was upset by the business of the Council?' Corbett persisted with his questioning. 'Nothing!' Bruce barked. 'Nothing of import. I wondered why it was called, just to discuss some Galloway baron imprisoned in England. There were petitions drafted for his release. Only the Good Christ knows why we met for that. The King arrived sullen but then something happened. I don't know what but suddenly he was like a child with a new toy. He was merry, drank deeply and said he was off to Kinghorn. And so he went. Why do you ask that? Benstede was there. He must have told you.' Bruce stopped and pursed his lips. 'Mind you, Benstede left much earlier. So perhaps he was not aware of the King's departure.' 'Were the French envoys there, my Lord?'

'Yes, de Craon, fawning and pleasant, urging the King to go to Kinghorn "pour l'amour". The stupid bastard! Of course, he denied it all later. So, Master Clerk, our King is dead and whom will your King support?' 'His Grace, King Edward,' Corbett replied slowly, 'will respect the wishes of the community of Scotland.' 'A pity,' Bruce murmured so quietly that Corbett could hardly hear him. 'I always thought that if Alexander died without an heir, Edward would support the house of Bruce!' He stopped speaking and gazed hard at Corbett and then continued quietly, almost as if he was talking to himself. 'I fought in the Holy Land for the Cross, and in England for Edward against the rebels; I have founded monasteries, supported Holy Mother Church so God would exalt my family. I watched Alexander whore, drink, lecher and toady to your Edward and I knew that I was a better man. In 1238 Alexander III's father promised me the crown but then he married again and begat Alexander, the third of that name, and the cup was dashed from my lips. Then Alexander became king, with no living heir and married his French paramour, lusting after her, proclaiming he would beget an heir. Well,' Bruce suddenly stopped, recollecting where he was and to whom he was speaking. He stared dully at Corbett. 'Get out, Master Corbett!' he waved his hand. 'Go! Go now!' Corbett nudged the gawking Ranulf, rose, bowed and, followed by Bruce's retainers, swept out of the room.

The retinue accompanied Corbett and Ranulf out of Leith and on to the now darkening track to Edinburgh. They exchanged insults with Ranulf and then turned back. Corbett heaved a sigh of relief, told Ranulf to keep his questions to himself and, head down, rode quietly along turning over in his mind what Bruce had told him. An angry, embittered man, Corbett concluded, who had no love for King Alexander. Indeed, he had good cause to benefit from his death, yet, Corbett reasoned, he was only one among many.

It was dark when they reached the outskirts of Edinburgh. Corbett relaxed, the thoroughfare was busy as carts, traders and farmers trudged home. Suddenly there was a commotion, confusion and curses as an empty cart overturned, the horse plunging and rearing in its traces with no sign of the driver. Corbett and Ranulf, riding abreast, stopped and gazed at the chaos. Two figures who had been walking ahead of them, suddenly turned and came sauntering back. Corbett saw them and straightened in his saddle. There was something wrong. He caught a glimpse of steel. He grabbed the reins of Ranulf's garron, and kicked his own into a canter. The two men were knocked aside as Corbett swung round the overturned wagon and broke into a gallop, clinging to his horse and hoping it would keep its feet on the rough rutted track. As soon as they were amongst the shuttered houses of Edinburgh, Corbett slowed down and turned to grin at the pale, terrified face of Ranulf. 'Don't ask me who they were,' he said. 'I don't know. They may have even been friendly but I remembered the old saying, "On a dark lonely road, one never meets a friend".' Ranulf nodded and promptly vomited, leaning over his horse's head as his stomach gave vent to its sudden fear. Corbett smiled; a few minutes later he wished he hadn't, for he too was sick and was still trembling when they safely reached the abbey gates.

NINE

The next morning the Prior brought a letter for Corbett; a simple note which said that Benstede had been attacked by unknown assailants the previous morning, that he was safe but advised Corbett to be most cautious. Corbett quietly vowed he would. He washed, dressed and took Ranulf down to the refectory for bread, cheese, a little ripe fruit and some watered wine. Afterwards, he ensured the men who had accompanied him to Scotland were well before sending Ranulf off to wash their clothes and busy himself about the abbey.

Corbett returned to his cell, carefully bolted the door and drew from a large leather pouch, parchment, pumice-stone, inkhorn, quill pens, a long thin razor-edged knife and a wad of red sealing-wax. He unrolled the parchment, scrubbed it with the pumice-stone and gently blew the fragments away, dipped his quill into the unclasped inkhorn and began to draft a letter to Burnell. It took hours and it was not until the late afternoon that he began the final copy.

'Hugh Corbett, clerk to Robert Burnell, Bishop of Bath and Wells, Chancellor, greetings. I have continued to stay at the Abbey of Holy Rood involved in the matter assigned to me. Let me first say that rumour and gossip abound, many shadows but so far very little substance. Common report now believes that Alexander III, King of Scotland, accidentally fell to his death from Kinghorn Ness on 18th March 1286. The King had convened a special meeting of the Council to discuss the imprisonment of a Galloway baron in England. The meeting was attended by the principal barons, both lay and ecclesiastic, of the kingdom. The King came in, sullen and withdrawn, but his mood changed rapidly. The business of the Council was soon dealt with and merged into general feasting when the King surprised everyone by announcing he intended to join the Queen at Kinghorn. Many remonstrated with him for a howling storm was raging outside, it was night and the journey was a dangerous one. The King brushed this opposition aside and left, taking two body squires with him, Patrick Seton and Thomas Erceldoun. They rode to Queensferry and persuaded the master boatman, against his better judgement, to ferry them across the Firth of Forth to Inverkeithing. They arrived safely and were met by the royal purveyor from Kinghorn (also called Alexander) who had brought horses down to the beach for the royal party; these included the King's favourite, a white mare called Tamesin which he had left at Kinghorn for the Queen's own use. The purveyor also attempted to reason with the King but to no avail. His Grace rode off. One of the grooms, Seton (a reputed lover of the King), knew the paths well and, in the darkness, somehow got far in advance of the King and so reached Kinghorn Manor. Erceldoun fared much worse. He could not control his horse which finally bolted so he and the royal purveyor stayed drinking in Inverkeithing. Meanwhile, King Alexander reached the top of Kinghorn Ness where both rider and horse toppled over the cliff to their deaths.

The next morning a search-party found the corpses on the sand below. The King's neck was broken, his face almost unrecognisable, his body a mass of bruises. The royal physician dressed the corpse for burial and it was interred eleven days later at Jedburgh. A Council of Regency was set up to supervise affairs: the Queen is pregnant and, if nothing comes of it, the Council will ensure that the crown of Scotland passes to Alexander III's granddaughter, Princess Margaret of Norway. However, there are others, notably the Bruces, who are more than prepared to advance their own claims to the throne. The real subject of my mission is the death of Alexander and certain conclusions can now be reached regarding it:

Item – Alexander III was well-known for his mad galloping around the countryside in pursuit of some lady. There is no reason why he should treat a new bride any different.

Item – On the night of March 18th, there was a fierce storm; Alexander was not drunk but he had been drinking heavily. Moreover, he was riding a dangerous path. It may well be pointed out that he could have taken a safer route but this was not possible. Kinghorn is near the waters of the Forth, its most accessible route is the cliff-top track. The King could have ridden further inland, but he would have lost his way on the wild, grassy moorland which conceals marsh and bog to trap the unwary traveller. Consequently, Alexander followed the usual route, albeit in very dangerous circumstances. There may be a number of explanations for Alexander's death.

Item – It was an accident. The King's horse, given all the conditions described above, could well have slipped and tumbled over the cliffs, taking his rider with him.

Item – It may have been brought about by negligence. The purveyor, Alexander, is a drunkard. He could have resented being called out on such a dark, stormy night, not saddled the King's horse properly and this caused the accident on Kinghorn Ness. Yet, if this is so, why did the accident not happen earlier? And would such negligence have taken both horse and rider over the cliff's edge?

Item – Did Alexander III die on Kinghorn Ness or was it some cunning stratagem of the King? Alexander III was known for his love of disguises, masques and jests. Did he arrange his mock death for some secret reason? I appreciate that this is a fantasy and there is no real proof for it. Moreover, the accident occurred over two months ago and no one has any reason to refute the obvious, that the King is dead and lies buried at Jedburgh Abbey.

Item – King Alexander III was murdered by Person or Persons unknown though for what reasons, and by what means, are still a mystery. A number of unexplained factors make this a possibility.

Item – Why did the King leave Edinburgh on such a night just to be with his Queen? He could have waited till the morning. If it was lust, there were other ladies ready and willing. If it was love, why was Queen Yolande so calm and not grief-stricken by his death?

Item – The King arrived sullen to the Council meeting, convened for the most petty of reasons, then suddenly his mood changed, he became joyful, happy as a groom on his wedding night. What happened to cause this?

Item – The most mysterious aspect of this is that there is no evidence that when the King came to the Council meeting he intended to leave but decided to do so there and then. However, messages had already been sent to Kinghorn instructing the purveyor to be on the beach with horses ready for the King, hours before the Council convened. Who sent these orders and how did they cross the Forth?

Finally, there are the prophecies of Alexander's imminent death which were circulating weeks before his death. What were the sources of these predictions? If it was murder (and I have slender evidence that it was) then, my Lord, let us remember Cicero's question – "Cui bono".? Who would profit from it? Bruce, bitter at the crown being taken from him in 1238? Resentful at Alexander and fearful that the King might beget an heir by his new queen and so lose for a second time the opportunity to advance the claims of his own house?

Yolande, his queen, who could not even be bothered to inspect her dead husband's corpse but keeps herself closeted at Kinghorn, claiming she is pregnant? She knew her husband was coming that evening but, when he failed to arrive, did not even bother to send out any search-party to look for him.

Patrick Seton, the King's squire and body-servant. He loved Alexander the King as a man loves a woman. He was jealous of Yolande and was the only person with the King when he died. I do wonder if the King's mad gallop through a storm-blown night finally unhinged his mind and so he caused the King's death and later died of a broken heart? I cannot understand why, after arriving at Kinghorn, he refused to wait up for his royal master and did not go looking for the King. Did he know his master was already dead?

The French, too, gained great advantage from the death of Alexander. Their new king, Philip IV, is devoting all his energies and resources to building up alliances in Europe. Alexander, God knows for what reason, always spurned them; now he is gone, Philip can weave fresh webs, gain an ally with a knife at England's back. Perhaps he also hoped, and still does, that our Liege Lord, King Edward, will be drawn into Scottish affairs and so divert resources England might have used in protecting her possessions in Gascony.

There is our sly, secretive Father in Christ, Bishop

Wishart. A close adviser of the dead King, he now wields power because of that King's death. Why was he (and it must have been him) so quick in sending off horsemen early on the morning of 19th March to check on the King's safety? Did he already know something was wrong? Unfortunately I cannot question him or, as yet, the men he sent who actually discovered the King's corpse.

Of course, and I hesitate to broach the matter, the English may have arranged Alexander III's death but to what advantage? There are other and better suspects. Edward is involved in France and I can see no profit for him in the death of an ally.

Other problems obscure the issue; whoever killed Alexander must surely have got to the ferry first, crossed the Firth of Forth, knew the route the King was to take, carried out their plan and got away, hoping the King's companions would not discover this. And done all this in the blackness of night? The Good God knows I would dismiss the matter as fanciful and accept that the Scottish King died of an accidental fall from his horse except for what I found, those little shreds clinging to a thorn bush on Kinghorn Ness crying out "Murder" to the world. Even if there is an answer for these, other questions still remain beating like blood about my head. They can only be resolved at great danger to myself and so I beg you, my Lord, to order my withdrawal from this country for Satan walks here. It is a bubbling pot and soon it will boil and spill over, scalding and burning all who are near it. My life and that of Benstede are under threat from God knows whom, for people believe we are here on a secret mission connected with the succession to the Scottish throne. I beg you to keep this in mind. God save you. Written on 18th June 1286 at the Abbey of Holy Rood.'

Corbett sat and studied the letter he had written.

Darkness fell and he put the report away while he lay on his bed and considered its contents. There must be, he thought, some key, some crack in this mystery he could use to achieve an answer. He remembered the old adage from his studies, "If a problem exists then a logical solution must also exist. It is only a matter of time before you find it". If you find it, Corbett added bitterly to himself. He felt he was involved in some royal masque, a diversion, a play where he was one of the mummers, blundering around in the dark to the silent laughter of an audience who always stayed in the shadows. Hasty rides at midnight along windswept cliffs, a King falling into darkness, prophecies of doom. Corbett reconsidered the prophecies. Surely, if he could find this source then he might find a lot more? If the prophecies were innocent, then who was responsible and, more importantly, who ensured other people knew about them? Corbett tried to think back, unravelling the skein of information he had gathered. Someone had named the Prophet? Someone called Thomas? Thomas the Rhymer – Thomas of Learmouth. Corbett swung his legs off the bed and, with a tinder, lit the room's three large candles, took out Burnell's letter and sealed it. He decided it would go as it was written while he proceeded with other matters.

The abbey bells rang for vespers but Corbett waited till he heard the monks returning from the chapel, before going down to join Ranulf in the whitewashed refectory. A plain meal of bread, soup and watered wine was served while one of the brothers read from the Scriptures. Corbett sat impatiently throughout, his only consolation being the amusement he derived from Ranulf's face as he ate his simple food amidst such sanctified surroundings. Once the meal was over and the thanksgiving intoned, Corbett whispered to Ranulf to return to their chamber while he sought an interview with the Prior. The latter readily agreed, inviting Corbett to walk with him in the silent, shadowy cloisters, taking advantage of the first soft breezes of early summer. For a while they strolled in silence before Corbett began to ask the Prior about his vocation to the monastic life, enjoying the sardonic replies and surprised to find that the Prior was both a distant kinsman to Robert Bruce and a keen herbalist, interested in medicine, with a passion for concocting simples, potions and cures. Corbett gently led the conversation on to the late King and was surprised at the outburst he drew. 'A good, strong ruler,' the Prior commented, 'but as a man, well ...' his voice trailed off, leaving the silence to be broken only by the sound of his sandalled feet pattering against the slabstones. 'What do you mean?' Corbett asked. 'I mean,' the Prior heatedly retorted, 'he was a lecher, who forsook his duties. For ten, eleven years he was a widower with every opportunity to marry and beget a son. Instead, he pursues his lusts, marries late and then dies in pursuit of that lust, leaving Scotland without an heir.' Corbett noted that the bitter anger deep within the Prior was about to well over and tactfully he remained silent. 'Even here,' the Prior continued, 'in the Abbey of the Holy Rood, he pursued his lusts! A young noblewoman, a widow on a journey to her late husband's grave, but the King came and saw her. He pursued her, showering her with gifts, jewels and precious cloths. Then he seduced her, not in his castle or one of his manors but here in open defiance of his vows and ours. I remonstrated with him but he just laughed in my face.' The Prior paused. 'A fitting end,' he commented. 'God save him and pity him. I should have attended that Council meeting you know?' he added more lightly, 'but I was busy, I sent my excuses. Who knows, perhaps I could have prevailed with him.' He lapsed into silence and

Corbett, stealing a sideways glance, noted, even in the shadowy moonlight, how tense and bitter the Prior had become. 'Father,' Corbett cautiously asked, 'you say the King almost brought about his own death?' The Prior pursed his lips and nodded. 'Then,' Corbett continued, 'did others think that? I mean, would this be the source of the many prophecies that some evil would befall the King?' The Prior shrugged and continued to walk, his hand leaning gently on Corbett's arm. 'Yes,' he answered. 'People did think the King acted rashly but there were other prophecies, not just pious speculation. These were uttered by that strange creature, Thomas the Rhymer, or Thomas of Learmouth.' 'Why strange?' 'In both appearance and ways. He is for ever issuing his four-line stanzas predicting the future for individuals or even entire families. A strange man with a mysterious past. There are rumours that he disappeared for nine years in Elfland!' 'Could I meet him?' Corbett asked brusquely. 'Is it possible?' The Prior turned and smiled thinly. 'I wondered why you wanted to speak to me. Thomas is a minor laird; he holds land near Earlston in Roxburghshire. I know him, I have even protected him on a number of occasions against scurrilous attacks by fellow priests.' He stopped and put a hand on Corbett's shoulder. 'I will write to him and see what I can do, but be careful, Hugh, be very careful!'

Corbett, stealing a sideways glance, noticed, even in the shadowy moonlight, how tense and taut the Prior had become. 'Father,' Corbett cautiously asked, 'you say the King claimed he thought about his own death?' The Prior pursed his lips and nodded. 'Then,' Corbett continued, 'did others think that this meant, would this be the source of the many prophecies that spoke of the death of the King?' The Prior shrugged and continued to walk, his hand resting gently on Corbett's arm. 'Yes,' he answered. 'People did think the King acted rashly but there were other prophecies, not just pious speculation. These were uttered by that strange creature, Thomas the Rhymer, or Thomas of Learmouth.' 'Why strange?' 'In both appearance and ways. He is for ever issuing his formidable stanzas predicting the future for individuals or even entire families. A strange man with a mysterious past. There are rumours that he disappeared for nine years in Elfland.' 'Could I meet him?' Corbett asked curiously. 'Is it possible?' The Prior turned and smiled thinly. 'I wondered why you wanted to speak to me. Thomas is a minor laird; he holds land near Earlston in Roxburghshire. I know him. I have even protested on a number of occasions against scurrilous attacks on fellow priests.' He stopped and put a hand on Corbett's shoulder. 'I will write to him and see what I can do, but be careful, Hugh, be very careful!'

TEN

The next morning, the Prior, true to his word, immediately sent off a courier to Thomas of Learmouth whilst Corbett despatched one of his retinue with his letter to Burnell. Corbett had been accompanied north by four messengers – chosen by the Chancellor from his own household. They had stayed in the abbey kicking their heels and helping with administrative tasks to pay their way; now, one of them was only too happy to take the letter and ride south with Corbett's instructions ringing in his ears. After that Corbett just had to wait, pleased to rest and stay in the monastery where he felt secure and safe. He studied the draft of the report he had sent to Burnell and re-examined it, going over time and again all he had learnt since his arrival in Scotland. The more he analysed the events surrounding King Alexander's death, the more certain he became it was murder. But by whom? And how? Corbett felt hemmed in by the sheer frustration of the task assigned him. He gave Ranulf a brief description of what had happened but his servant, with a keen sense of survival, immediately tried to link events to the men who had attempted to attack them on the road from Leith. Ranulf believed the French were responsible; Corbett at first agreed, but then queried why they had waited so long and privately concluded that the attackers were from Lord Bruce's retinue.

The days passed, the monks celebrated the Feast of Midsummer, the beheading of St. John the Baptist. Corbett attended the solemn High Mass in the Abbey church watching the celebrants in their blood-red and gold robes moving like figures in a dream amidst the constant plumes of fragrant incense. The melodious chant of the monks intoning the psalm caught his ear, "Exsurge Domine, Exsurge et vindica causam meam" – "Arise, O Lord, arise, and judge my cause". Corbett closed his eyes and made his own prayer, sending it up into the void. Did God really care that the Lord's Anointed, blessed with royal oils on hands, feet and brow, the descendant of St. Margaret with the blood of Edward the Confessor in his veins, had been destroyed, brought low, murdered, tossed off the top of a cliff like a spent leaf blown in the wind? Corbett realised the dangers of what was happening, he was becoming obsessed with this matter as he did with anything he could not solve, rationalise, arrange in neat columns. He must make some progress, he thought, impose some order on the chaos which faced him or Burnell would not need to order his departure from Scotland. He would leave of his own accord and accept the consequences.

Therefore Corbett was relieved when, five days after his departure, the Prior's courier returned bearing an oral message. 'Thomas of Learmouth would only be too pleased to receive Hugh Corbett, clerk to the royal chancery of England.' 'Oh,' the Prior added almost as an afterthought, 'the courier also brought a personal message from Thomas.' 'What do you mean?' Corbett enquired. 'I have never met him and we know nothing of each other!' The Prior shrugged. 'It was nothing, just – "Tell Hugh that the pain Alice caused will disappear in time".' The Prior scrutinised Corbett's surprised face. 'What does it mean, Hugh? Who is Alice?' Corbett just shook his head and slowly walked away. He thought of Alice, beautiful Alice atte Bowe, the leader of a coven in London which had plotted against the King. He, Corbett, had destroyed the conspiracy and sent Alice to the fires at Smithfield. The very mention of her name awoke old pains; it was only much later on that he began to wonder how Thomas knew about Alice atte Bowe.

The next day, with a lay brother as a guide, Corbett and Ranulf left the abbey and journeyed south. The weather had changed; summer in its glorious profusion of colours had transformed the land that Corbett had travelled through a few weeks before. A blue sky with white lacy clouds, green, blue-dashed moors and grasslands, the hills strewn with wild flowers of many colours and different hues. It was wild countryside, steep hills and grassy plateaux, scarred and gashed by steel-grey rocks and rapid, frothing rivers which tumbled down the hillside. The lay brother, a simple soul, could name the flowers, the different varieties of heather and the birds which wheeled and soared with joy above them: he also taught Ranulf a song in broad Scots about the dangers of being a young girl alone on the moors with a young gallant. The song and their laughter were so infectious that Corbett joined in. They travelled for days and on the third entered the Lauderdale valley. The lay brother pointed below to the rounded ivy-covered tower, the centre of a small peel-castle nestling on the banks of the Lauder River. 'Thomas the Rhymer's castle,' he commented. 'Come. Let us go down.'

As they approached, Corbett realised the fortifications of Earlston were a square tower of pleasing proportions within a stockade or peel which Corbett had seen many times on his journeys into Scotland. It was surrounded by a moat spanned by a fragile bridge which they cantered across as quickly as possible into a dusty courtyard. This was small, containing a deep draw-well, stable, byre and storehouses, the latter no more than lean-to erections of timber plastered with clay. A groom ran forward to hold their horses while another ambled off to tell Sir Thomas of their arrival. Corbett dismounted and looked around, noting that the tower was not as vulnerable as would at first appear: narrow slits pierced the walls and a machicolation jutted out from the parapet just above the tower door from where defenders could hurl stones, or boiling oil, on any attackers.

Corbett was about to investigate further when he heard Ranulf's panic-struck voice. 'Master Corbett! Master Corbett! Come quickly! It's Sir Thomas!' Corbett turned to see a tall, lank, white-haired man in a black robe standing in front of their horses. Corbett strode across and the figure turned to greet him. Corbett stopped, shocked. 'Sir Thomas?' he queried. 'Yes, Hugh, it's Sir Thomas of Learmouth.' Corbett stared. The man's hair was white, as was his skin, but his eyes and lips were a bright pink, in fact the eyes were blue but pink-rimmed and, more strange, bereft of lashes. Corbett remembered he had heard of this type of man, an "Albus", an all-white man or albino. He tried to conceal his astonishment but Sir Thomas was almost laughing at him. 'Come, Hugh, say you are surprised. Most people are. I am odd? Different?' His voice was clear, low and pleasing.

Corbett grinned back; a Welshman had once told him that each person has an aura about him, be it good or evil, which goes out to other people. If this was so then Sir Thomas exuded friendship and goodwill. 'What matter the face or head,' he quoted, 'it is the heart which counts!' 'You like poetry, Master Corbett?' 'I enjoy it when I can.' Good,' Sir Thomas replied. 'We knew you were coming,' he added for effect, and laughed at Ranulf's gaping face. 'No gift of prophecy,' he jabbed a finger upwards. 'I saw you from the top of the tower. Come. Food is ready!' They entered the cool, dark tower, across stone-vaulted floors and climbed up a narrow twisting staircase into the hall. A sombre stone chamber, its walls were adorned with green velvet drapes while a polished table with benches on either side stood in the middle of the rush-strewn floor. At the far end was a narrow door which, Thomas announced, led into the kitchen. A small, dark, smiling woman appeared through it. Thomas put his arm round her shoulders and introduced his wife Bethoe, who gently murmured her welcome. She bade them sit and brought a tray of wine, cups, and a bowl of sugared wafers. They ate, talking about the journey and the gossip of the court until Thomas asked Bethoe to show Ranulf and the lay brother to their quarters. Once they were gone, he turned to Corbett and stared fixedly with his terrible, haunting eyes. 'Well, Master Corbett? What does an English clerk want with me?' Corbett set his goblet down before replying. 'His Grace, Alexander III. He died, as you know, from a fall on Kinghorn Ness. You prophesied his death.' Thomas nodded. 'How did you know?' Corbett asked. 'I saw it,' Thomas replied, touching his forehead lightly with his fingers. 'I saw pictures. Images, when I looked into the water.' 'What water?' Corbett snapped. 'The small, dark people,' Thomas smiled. 'Some people call them fairies, goblins. The Romans called them the "Picti" or Picts, the "Painted People".' He grinned, his teeth white and even. 'The stories are true. I lived with them, not for nine years, but for a while. They are outcasts. So am I, and we share the same gift of glimpsing the future.'

Corbett sighed and shook his head in disbelief. Thomas turned and pointed to a fly crawling on the end of the table. 'Look at the fly; all he can feel, all he can see is the table. Can he be blamed for believing that the only things which exist are himself and the table? So it is with us, Master Corbett. We only believe what we can see and touch!' 'I have heard a similar philosophy enunciated by the schoolmen,' Corbett rejoined, 'but, seeing into the future?' Thomas rose and beckoned Corbett over to one of the arrow-slit windows and pointed down to the winding River Lauder. 'Look, Master Corbett, from here we can see all the river in our view, but if we were in a boat on that river, what would we see? A little in front, a little to the rear and the banks on either side. So it is with time. It is simply a matter of where you stand!'

Corbett turned away and picked up the goblet, tasting the full red flavour of Bordeaux. 'So, where do you stand to get a glimpse of the future, to see the death of kings?' 'Sometimes I just know,' sighed Thomas. 'But Alexander's death, I saw it in the water, in the reflecting bowl.' 'I don't understand. What did you see?' Corbett asked with puzzlement. 'The King and a horse falling clear against the night sky,' Thomas replied. 'That is all?' Corbett asked. 'That is all! Why, should there be more,' asked Thomas. 'But,' protested Corbett, 'you predicted the actual day.' 'No, I did not,' Thomas retorted. 'I openly told the King that the Day of Judgement was near. It was only after the event that people ascribed an actual day.' Thomas looked quizzically at Corbett. 'You believe that the King was murdered, don't you?' The clerk nodded. 'Yes,' he admitted ruefully. 'I believe he was murdered, but how and why and by whom I do not know! Perhaps you can tell me that!' Thomas laughed softly. 'No, I only see pictures, images, not their many causes or what follows because of it.

But,' he continued seriously, 'I do see danger for you and I also feel sorry, as you have come a long way for nothing.' He crossed over to Corbett and put a hand on his shoulder. 'You must find the truth, Master Corbett. Yes, I told the King of imminent danger but, given the way he charged round his kingdom in the dead of night, even the court fool could have warned him just as accurately.' Thomas turned and looked out of the window. 'Because you have come so far, Hugh, tomorrow I will take you to see the Painted Men, the little people, the fairies, goblins, Picts, or whatever you wish to call them.' Thomas looked at Corbett. 'You will come?' Corbett nodded. 'Good!' Thomas exclaimed and clapped his hands. 'Then let us eat!'

Late the next morning Corbett and Thomas left Earlston and struck south-west for the great Forest of Ettrick. Ranulf and the lay brother were left behind as Thomas explained that the Picti were secretive people, hostile to those races who had pushed them from their lands and so did not take kindly to strangers. As they rode, Thomas told Corbett more about the Picti, how they had once ruled Scotland, even launching raids across the great Roman wall to the south to pillage and plunder Rome's colonies. 'Their culture,' Thomas explained, 'is ancient. They came out of the darkness and worshipped it, calling the earth their Mother-God. They built their great fortresses on high places, rings of rocks enclosing courts and small timbered housing.'

Corbett and Thomas were now riding across open meadowland and the poet pointed to three hills, black and stark against the summer-blue sky. 'The Eldon Hills,' he pointed out. 'Where the Picts had their own fort. It was there I first met them, a small hunting-party. I tended the wounds of one of their men and they took me back with them into the great Forest of Ettrick.' Thomas smiled.

'Because of that, the superstitious say I met the fairies and went to live with them for nine years. Very few people,' he concluded, 'have seen the Picts and because of their colouring, size and silent ways, it is easy to understand why folk call them pixies, goblins or elves.' Corbett listened, fascinated by the legends about these secret people. He had heard similar stories amongst the Welsh and told Thomas about them. The conversation then turned to the legends of King Arthur and Thomas discussed the epic poem he was writing, "Sir Tristram", asking Corbett to tell him all he knew about Wales.

ELEVEN

They spent that evening at the Cistercian monastery of Melrose and continued their journey the following morning. The countryside became more deserted, farmsteads and villages more sparse as they approached the green mass of trees on the far horizon which Corbett knew must be the great Forest of Ettrick. They drew near the trees and Corbett felt he was entering a different world. At first it was cool and beautiful, the sun's rays piercing the trees and shimmering on the gorse and heather like light through the coloured glass of a cathedral window. Then it became darker, the trees denser, thicker, hemming them in on all sides as Thomas guided their horses along some secret path known only to him. The birdsong, so clear at the edge of the forest, was now quiet. Small creatures moved and stirred amongst the undergrowth, the snapping of twigs and mysterious rustling noises sounding all the more ominous in the green cold silence of the forest. A boar, tusked and red-eyed, suddenly burst from the undergrowth and Corbett jumped in fear as it blundered its way amongst the trees. Still, they went further, even Thomas was quiet; the tension became oppressive, now and again broken by the mocking call of some bird.

Corbett pushed his horse nearer to Thomas. 'Are we

following the right route?' he whispered anxiously. Thomas nodded. 'Wait,' he muttered. 'I will show you.' They rode further on and Thomas pointed to a copper beech. Corbett peered closer and saw a V-rod and crescent marked on the tree. 'We are following the right path,' Thomas said, 'and soon we will be there.' He rode, Corbett following, noting the same symbol appeared on other trees they passed. Then a low, warbling birdsong came clear and pure through the silence. Thomas stopped and gestured Corbett to do the same. 'Do not move,' he whispered. The whistle came again, stronger, almost threatening, and Thomas, pursing his lips, returned the call, raising his hands like a priest giving a benediction. The whistling came again, clear and simple, then abruptly ceased. Corbett looked into the green darkness, straining his eyes to see any movement and almost screamed with terror as a hand touched his leg. He looked down and saw a man, small, dark, with black hair flowing down to his shoulders, staring up at him. Corbett looked wildly around and saw others. Small, swarthy men, no higher than his chest-bone, dressed in leather jerkins and leggings. Some wore cloaks clasped at the neck with huge ornamental brooches. They were all armed with spears, short bows and wicked little daggers pushed into their belts. They stared impassively at Corbett while their leader talked to Thomas in a tongue that Corbett did not know, though it sounded like birdsong, high, clicking and quick. The chieftain then stopped speaking and bowed to Corbett, who felt the group around him suddenly relax. The leader took the bridle of Thomas's horse, another seized Corbett's and they were led deeper into the forest.

Corbett expected the Pictish village to be hidden and secretive but suddenly the trees thinned, the sunlight glimmered then poured through as they abruptly left the canopy of trees and entered a large clearing. A huge rocky outcrop at the far end jutted up and beneath it a small river or burn flowed quietly, turning and twisting as it followed its banks. The houses were scattered around, low-slung, timbered, with a thatched roof and small porch; it was a village scene similar to many Corbett had seen elsewhere except for the small dark people, their furtive looks and quiet ways. 'Come Corbett!' Thomas called. 'We are amongst friends.' 'Their language is strange,' Corbett said. 'And their ways are so secretive!' Thomas looked around and nodded. 'Once they were a proud people and ruled the greater part of Scotland but the Celts, the Angles, the Saxons and the Normans drove them from their lands into the dark vastness of the forests. They scarcely venture out and do not take easily to strangers.' 'And if I met them when I was alone?' Corbett asked. Thomas grimaced. 'Out in the open? They would pass you by. You would not see them here in the forest. If you injured or offended them,' Thomas turned and pointed to the carvings on the rocky outcrop, a woman with large generous thighs and huge round breasts, 'they would put you in a wicker basket and burn you alive, an offering to their Mother Goddess.' He saw Corbett frown and added, 'Come, Hugh, tell me what happens at your Smithfield?' Corbett stared at him and looked away, the tension between them broken by the Pictish leader who took Thomas by the hand, like a child with a parent, and led him into the largest house, beckoning Corbett to follow them.

Inside it was dark and cool, smelling faintly of crushed grass and heather. A fire burnt in a ring of stones in the centre, the smoke rising to a flue-hole in the roof above the rough timbered rafters. Corbett shuddered when he looked closer and saw human skulls nestling in the cross-pieces. An old man, swathed in robes, sat before the fire; he looked up when Corbett and Thomas squatted before him across the stones, peering at them with rheumy eyes, his lips parted in a toothless, dribbling smile. His face was so dark and wizened that he reminded Corbett of a monkey he had once seen in the royal menagerie in the Tower of London. Beer made from barley, and flat oat-cakes were brought for them. They ate in silence, Corbett conscious of the old man staring at them now joined by the leader who had met them in the forest. Once they had eaten, the fire was doused and branches laid across the stones. On these, a huge hanging bowl was placed, made of beaten copper decorated around the rim with birds pecking at ornamental roundels, dogs' heads, and a variety of animals, all lifelike in careful, exquisite craftsmanship. The bowl was filled with water and the old man, chanting softly to himself, poured powder into it from small leather pouches. The leader rose and brought Corbett a cup and, making signs, urged Corbett to drink the creamy goats' milk laced with something acrid which burnt his mouth and the back of his throat.

The old man continued to chant and Corbett suddenly felt more relaxed. The old man's wizened face lost its folds and wrinkles, the eyes firmed, clear blue in their trance-like stare. Corbett looked away and gazed around; the room had grown larger; he turned and saw Thomas smiling at him as if through a haze. 'Look into the bowl, Hugh, see what you like!' Corbett stared down into the water. A face rushed up to meet him, clear and lifelike; he stared into the sweet round face of his long-dead wife. He went to touch the water but someone grabbed his hand. Next his child appeared, then others long dead. Alice, black hair flowing around her beautiful face: other images arose clear and bright in all their colours. Corbett forgot about those around him so intent was he on watching the water. 'The King's Grace,' he muttered. 'Kinghorn!' The water cleared and another image appeared, a horse and rider, falling slowly from the edge of rocks. The horse was white, the rider cloaked, but his red hair streamed out against the darkness as he fell, open-mouthed, eyes staring into the black void.

Corbett felt a bitter taste at the back of his mouth and struggled to reassert himself, impose order on the chaos surrounding him. He looked up; the old wizened face was gone, instead the man was young, sharp-eyed, with long black hair falling to his shoulders. Corbett peered. 'Who are you?' he asked. 'My name is Darkness,' the man replied, the voice low, pleasant and perfectly understandable. Corbett gazed into the eyes and sensed something evil; whatever Thomas said, there was a malevolence here. These small, dark people were not just primitive tribesmen but held something old, ancient and evil. Corbett tried to assert himself once more. Logic. Reason. These were needed here. His task, he thought impatiently; Burnell would be waiting. There were problems but no solutions. He thought of Cicero. 'Cui bono?' he asked. 'Who profits from the King's death?' 'Look into the bowl, Clerk,' the voice was deeper, almost snapping, as if the speaker sensed Corbett's inner conflict. Corbett looked again into the clear water. A creature appeared, a lion, red and huge, bounding up the narrow winding streets of Edinburgh, splashing through rivers of blood which poured from the castle. The lion turned, jaws slavering, eyes ablaze with fury and Corbett flinched as it came towards him, belly crouched, its tail twitching, its hind legs tense, then it sprang. Corbett looked up and tried to rise, the skulls in the cross-beam of the house opened their mouths and bellowed with laughter. He saw de Craon sitting in that dirty, miserable ale-house. Aaron, Benstede's man, glaring at him through the crowd at the banquet in the castle while Benstede looked reproachfully at him. Corbett knew he had to leave but the room was spinning around him and he fell gratefully into the gathering blackness.

When he awoke, he was lying on grass in the open air. He blinked and stretched, feeling relaxed and contented after a good night's sleep, although there was a bitterness at the back of his throat. He remembered the hut, the bowl of water and the terrifying visions of the night. He sat up and looked around; he was in open grassland, the horses were hobbled. Thomas was sitting, looking thoughtfully at him, a blade of grass between his teeth. Corbett turned and saw the edge of the forest behind them. 'You feel well, Hugh?' Thomas asked. Corbett nodded. 'But where are we? The village! The forest! Where are we?' Corbett asked in puzzlement. 'We left them,' Thomas said. 'That was yesterday. You slept the whole night. This morning I put you on your horse and we left.' Corbett nodded, rose and moved away; he emptied his bladder and went to a nearby stream to bathe his hands and face in the cold clear water. They tended to their horses and ate the flat, tasteless biscuits Thomas had brought with him before beginning their ride back. Corbett, remembering all he had seen the previous night, was more wary of Thomas: the evil he had experienced in that hut was nothing to take lightly. What had he learnt, he asked himself? There was something, petty but significant. He knew the red lion represented the House of Bruce but the blood? Was Bruce a regicide? Had he killed Alexander to get to the throne? Corbett turned to the silent Thomas. 'You saw the lion?' he asked. The poet nodded. 'I did,' he replied; 'and the cascading blood.' He looked sharply at Corbett. 'That does not make Bruce an assassin.' Thomas continued, 'You saw matters as they will

be, not as they are. I saw other things after you fainted.'
'What things?' The poet closed his eyes and recited.

Of Bruce's side a son shall come,
From Carrick's bower to Scotland's throne:
The Red Lion beareth he.
The foe shall wear the Lion down
A score of years but three.
Till red of England blood shall run
Burn of Bannock to the sea.

'What does that mean?' Corbett testily asked. Thomas smiled. 'I do not know, but the red lion is not the Lord Bruce nor indeed his son, the Earl of Carrick but actually refers to Carrick's son, Bruce's grandson, a boy of twelve,' Thomas sniffed as if to say, 'Make of it what you wish.'

They continued their journey, their conversation desultory as if each was aware of the tension which now separated them. They stopped at Melrose and arrived in Earlston the following morning. Corbett was pleased to see Ranulf, now bored with the simple delights of the countryside and just as eager as his master to leave and have done with it. Corbett courteously thanked his hosts and, gently brushing aside their invitations, insisted on leaving at once. They departed the same day, Corbett eager and anxious to be back in Edinburgh. He had learnt something valuable, though he still could not isolate it in his mind. The problem of the prophecies was solved albeit in a way he had scarce expected. After three days hard riding, Corbett and his party reached Edinburgh in the middle of a sudden summer thunderstorm which drenched them to the skin. Ranulf was sullen and angry at the pace Corbett set, forgetting his pleasure at travelling again in constant moans about his aching back and saddle-sore thighs. The lay brother was quiet, contenting himself with the dry comment that he had done enough penance to wipe a thousand years of purgatory from the debt his soul owed God.

They were all pleased to enter the great gates of Holy Rood Abbey though Corbett sensed there was something wrong. A groom came out to take their horses and, when he saw Corbett, immediately ran off leaving all three of them standing in the pouring rain. He returned with the Prior and a young, red-haired man dressed in half-armour. The Prior's long face was white with anxiety. He nodded at Ranulf and the lay brother then turned to Corbett. 'I'm sorry, Hugh,' he said almost in a half-whisper, 'your servant can stay with us but you must accompany this knight.' He turned and gestured to his companion. 'This is Sir James Selkirk. He has been with us since yesterday. He comes from Bishop Wishart with a warrant for your arrest.' 'On what charge?' Corbett snapped. The Prior looked fearful and swallowed nervously before speaking. 'On treason and murder! Oh, Hugh,' he said. 'I do not doubt your innocence but you must go and clear your name.' Corbett nodded, too confused and tired to ask for details. It must be a mistake, he thought, and then remembered he was a lowly English clerk in a foreign land. He remembered the Lawnmarket, the black, stark gibbets, the criminal being pulled there and tried hard to control his shivering. In good, fluent English tinged with a broad Scots accent, Selkirk told him to mount his horse. Once he did, the man bound Corbett's hands tightly to the saddlebow and, passing the rope under the horse's belly, also secured his ankles. More men, about six, appeared; their horses were led out and saddled. Corbett could only shout at Ranulf to stay and do nothing before Selkirk took him at a canter out of the abbey.

TWELVE

The journey was quick and bruising; Selkirk led them through the town, up the craggy rock and across the wooden drawbridge into Edinburgh Castle. Corbett, aching, soaking wet and nauseous from his rough ride was pulled off his horse and bundled along the side of the donjon keep. He tried protesting to Selkirk, who simply struck him across the mouth and pushed him through the metal-studded door. Corbett slipped and tripped as he was pushed down a flight of steep narrow steps which ran under the keep. It was dark and dank, the walls glistening with streaks of green water. When Corbett reached the bottom, a gaoler in dirty leather jerkin, leggings and boots, greeted him with a world-weary look and removed his cloak, belt and dagger. In broad Scots he asked Selkirk for his authority, the soldier flourished a piece of parchment and told him to hurry. The man sighed and, choosing a key from a ring which hung round his fat waist, waddled down a narrow, dimly-lit passage past a number of cells. He stopped by one, unlocked it and gestured to Corbett to enter. Selkirk pushed him in and made him squat on a stone ledge while he cut free his bound hands only to fasten gyves to his wrists and ankles; attached by chains to the wall; these allowed Corbett to move but quickly chafed his wrists and ankles. Selkirk stood, looked down at

Corbett and patted him on the head. 'There, Master English Clerk,' he jibed. 'Now, try and travel around Scotland!' He gave a mock bow, laughed and left the cell. The gaoler followed, locking the door behind him.

Corbett just sat staring at the wet walls: the cell was narrow and fetid, a grating high in the wall gave a little air and light. In the far corner was a bundle of wet straw which he assumed was the bed. He rose but found his chains would not let him even reach it, so he slumped on the ledge and wondered how long he would be detained. Treason and murder were the charges but what was his treachery and whom had he allegedly murdered? The grating above grew dark and Corbett began to shiver, he was still soaking wet from his journey and was now cold and hungry. The gaoler returned hours later with a cup of brackish water, a bowl of badly-cooked meat and hard, stale bread. Corbett devoured it hungrily while the gaoler watched impassively but, when Corbett tried to ask him a question, slapped him in the mouth, grabbed the bowl and waddled out of the cell. Corbett tried to sleep but could not and sat trembling, trying to compose his thoughts but it was useless, he could not calm himself. He heard a scrabbling at the foot of his cell door and two small dark shadows blocked the faint line of light as they squirmed under and scurried across the cell floor. More rats entered and Corbett lashed out with his legs, blind to the sharp gyves knifing into his ankles. The rats fled and Corbett fell back on the ledge, chest heaving, sobbing with anger and fear, his eyes fixed on the grating, praying for dawn.

It grew light, then the sun's rays pierced the cell. The gaoler returned and left a stoup of water. Corbett drank it, sitting in his own filth, eyes fixed on the grating, already dreading the night. He calmed himself, trying to understand why he was imprisoned and who was responsible. He comforted himself with the fleeting thought that at least he had met Sir James Selkirk, who had found Alexander III's corpse, and wryly concluded he would question him if the opportunity presented itself. Corbett concentrated on the mystery surrounding King Alexander's death but the visions he had seen in the Pictish village returned to haunt him. He slept for a while and was roughly awakened as the door was flung open and Selkirk entered. He loosened the gyves, dragged Corbett to his feet and bundled him through the door, along the passage and up the steps into the pure, clear air. Corbett turned to Selkirk. 'Where am I going?' he remonstrated. 'We are taking you, English, to see Bishop Wishart.' Corbett shook his head. 'I want my cloak, my dagger and belt,' he said. 'Hot food and some wine.' Selkirk grinned. 'You're a traitor,' he replied. 'You're a prisoner. You make no demands!' Corbett was tired and no longer cared. 'I am an accredited English envoy,' he bluffed. 'I demand my belongings and some victuals.' Selkirk nodded. 'Fine,' he muttered. 'It makes no difference. Come.' He led Corbett into the kitchens, a cook brought him ale and a dish of meat and vegetables. When he had eaten, Selkirk returned and tossed his possessions at him; Corbett gathered them up and followed Selkirk up rows of steps and into a small, darkened chamber.

At the far end, in a pool of light thrown by sconce-torches and a cluster of candles, sat a small, balding figure swathed in robes whom Corbett recognised as Wishart, Bishop of Glasgow. He looked up as Corbett entered. 'Come in, Master Clerk,' he called, throwing down the manuscript he had been studying. 'Come, Sir James, a stool for our guest!' Corbett sat while the Bishop poured him a cup of mulled, spiced wine; Selkirk sat alongside him, lounging in a chair. The Bishop began to tidy up the parchment rolls in front of him so Corbett, tired of the farce, rose and refilled his goblet. 'Your Lordship,' he snapped. 'You arrested me, imprisoned me, all without charge. I am clerk to the King's Bench of the royal court of England. I am also an accredited envoy of the English Chancellor.' Wishart smiled. 'Master Corbett,' he replied. 'I do not care if you are the King of England's brother. By what right do you travel round this realm questioning Scotsmen about the death of their sovereign? Who gave you that authority?' Corbett had dreaded this question, always knowing it would be asked. He shrugged to conceal his alarm. 'I am an envoy,' he answered. 'It is my task to collect information. Your envoys do the same in England.' Wishart smirked and leaned forward, steepling his fingers. 'You think our late King was murdered?' he asked. 'Yes, I do,' Corbett replied quickly. 'Yes, I believe he was murdered. I could lie, I could bluff, but what I told you is the truth. I know he was murdered but by whom or how, I could not say.' Wishart nodded and Corbett instinctively felt the strain lessen. 'Master Corbett,' the Bishop began. 'I believe His Grace was murdered and I really don't care!' He waved an admonitory finger at Corbett. 'Don't misunderstand me. Alexander was not the best of men, certainly not the ideal Christian knight but, as a king, he ruled Scotland well. He kept her free of foreign alliances, foreign wars, foreign involvement.' Wishart's voice became impassioned. 'The only thing I care for, Englishman, more than my family and my church, is Scotland. Alexander served her well but failed her by not producing an heir when he married that French hussy.' 'Queen Yolande is pregnant,' Corbett interrupted, intrigued by the Bishop's attitude. 'Queen Yolande,' Wishart emphasised, 'is not pregnant. That has been established; she will return to France and so dash any hope of a permanent alliance.' 'But the Queen was pregnant?' Wishart shook his head. 'No. It was what the doctors call a false pregnancy, probably brought on by her husband's sudden death, feelings of guilt. God knows what!' 'And this alliance?' Corbett queried. Wishart smiled. 'You did not know? Alexander was intrigued by the new French King Philip and his schemes for Europe. Yolande de Dreux was the first step in sealing a new alliance with France.' Wishart shrugged. 'It was a secret. One I did not like but Alexander was headstrong. He never forgave your King for insulting him.' 'When?' asked Corbett, genuinely bewildered. 'In 1278,' Wishart replied. 'At Westminster when your King was crowned. Edward I rightly asked Alexander to do fealty for lands he held in England and Alexander agreed but then the English asked Alexander to do homage for Scotland. Our King refused, justly claiming he held his throne direct of God. Alexander never forgave Edward the insult.' 'I did not know this,' murmured Corbett. 'But you said you, too, believed King Alexander III was murdered!' 'No,' Wishart replied carefully. 'I said he might have been. His violent death was only a matter of course given the way he lived. But, if he was murdered, the important thing is not who did it but why. If it was a personal vendetta.' The Bishop paused and shrugged. 'But if it was a political act then it affects Scotland and excites my interest.' 'Your Lordship does not seem to care,' Corbett interjected. 'His Lordship,' Wishart replied, 'cares very much. But what can I do? Ask for a full, public investigation? And what happens if it turned out to be the Lord Bruce – eh? What then, Master Clerk? Civil War? No, that is not the way.' 'So,' Corbett added. 'You are interested in what I find. So, why the prison and,' Corbett turned to Selkirk, 'the ministrations of this thing!'

Selkirk stiffened with anger and made to rise but

Wishart waved a hand at him. 'Yes, Corbett, I am very interested in what you find. Sir James and the prison cell were simply a warning not to go too far, not to presume too much on our present weakness.' 'And the charge of murder?' Corbett asked quietly. 'Oh,' the Bishop smiled. 'Thomas Erceldoun, the squire you so closely questioned on the night of our banquet. He was found garrotted in the church of St. Giles some seven days ago.' The Bishop stifled a yawn. 'He was a strong young man and I doubt if you could have murdered him. Anyway, we do know that on the day he was murdered you were some distance away from Edinburgh, but it was a good pretext to arrest and detain you should you attempt to complain to your masters in London!' Corbett sat and thought. Erceldoun was dead, that was significant, but he was too engrossed in what Wishart was saying to study the matter now. He was exhausted and wished to sleep. 'So,' he said wearily. 'What do you want from me?' 'Nothing yet,' Wishart replied. 'Except that I will not detain you in prison or expel you from Scotland, on one condition. You will tell me if you find it was murder and give me the name of the murderer. In return,' the Bishop straightened in his chair. 'I will give you every assistance. Sir James Selkirk,' he bowed at the knight beside Corbett, 'will assist you whenever you ask. What do you say, English Clerk?' Corbett tried to gather his wits. If he did not agree it would mean the end of his mission. If he accepted, then all it would mean was sharing some of his conclusions with Wishart. Corbett nodded. 'I accept your Lordship's offer but you must answer some questions first.' Wishart looked surprised but agreed. 'Certainly what questions?' 'You were at the Council meeting the night the King died?' Wishart nodded. 'Did you notice anything untoward? I do know the King's mood changed abruptly from one of moroseness to one of joy.

Do you know why?' Wishart shook his head. 'No, I too noted the King's change in mood but dismissed it for King Alexander was an excitable, changeable man. The Council meeting was called for petty reasons. I believe Seton was responsible but your own Benstede can answer for that, he and Seton seemed close friends. All I remember is that the King and de Craon were talking excitedly together and that de Craon seemed pleased. The rest you must know.'

Corbett stared at Wishart. He wanted to get away to think clearly. He knew why Wishart had him imprisoned then brought him here cold and tired: he hoped to ensnare him. Corbett suddenly grasped that the Bishop, like others, really believed he was here for other reasons and hoped to trap him into an admission. If not, then keep him busy searching for the murderer of Alexander III. Well, Corbett shrugged, he would continue in his task and then return to England. The succession to the Scottish throne was not his concern. Yet, there were still questions. 'In the days before his death,' he asked, 'did the King do anything out of character?' Wishart thought for a while and shook his head. 'No,' he replied. 'He was morose, ill-tempered. He was preparing to send his confessor, a Franciscan, Father John, to Rome on a certain private, personal mission which he did not discuss with me or the Council.' Corbett detected the air of injured pride in this priest who liked to know everything. 'Was Father John sent?' 'No,' Wishart replied. 'In fact, just before the King left for Kinghorn, he instructed me to order Father John not to go but stay at the castle till he returned. That is all.' Corbett rubbed his eyes wearily, feigning to be more exhausted than he really was. 'My Lord,' he said weakly. 'I really must sleep.' 'You are welcome to stay here,' Wishart replied. 'No. No. I must return to the Abbey. I would appreciate the protection of Sir James. Unfortunate accidents can happen to the unwary traveller.' 'True! True!' the Bishop exclaimed. 'It is dangerous to be imprudent. Sir James, if you would?' Selkirk nodded his consent and Corbett hurriedly took his leave of the Bishop.

The journey back was a silent if an uneventful one. After waking the guestmaster by tolling the abbey gate bell, Corbett was greeted by an anxious Prior and a solicitous Ranulf. He refused to answer their questions but calmed their anxieties, dismissing Sir James as if he was a page-boy with a gentle tap on his cheek. During the next two days Corbett stayed in his cell, recuperating from the journey and forced imprisonment. He did not discuss his ordeal with Ranulf or the Prior, although he told them time and again that all was well and let them order his life, content to drift, think and reflect. He spent his time putting down on odd scraps of vellum his different thoughts on what he had learnt over the past few weeks. A pattern was emerging though it was vague and very ill-defined.

On the third evening after his return from the castle, he suddenly announced that he was going back to Kinghorn. Ranulf groaned in protest but Corbett, fully recovered, insisted that his servant pack and make the necessary preparations. He also instructed the two remaining messengers whom Burnell had sent with them, to accompany him fully-armed. He bought provisions from the abbey kitchen and informed the Prior that they would be away for at least two days. The Prior asked the reason for his journey. 'Confidentially,' said Corbett, 'I must see the Queen before she returns to France.' 'But she is enceinte!' the monk exclaimed. 'She cannot return!' 'If she was pregnant,' Corbett cryptically replied, 'she would not be allowed to leave.' The Prior simply shook his head in puzzlement and walked away.

THIRTEEN

Early the next morning, Corbett and his party left for Queensferry, fully armed. They encountered no opposition though Ranulf maintained that he had seen a rider watching them as they crossed the bridge at Dalmeny. Corbett heeded the warning, telling his companions to be most vigilant until they were across the Forth. They stabled their horses at the ferrymaster's house, paying for their fodder and keep until they returned. The ferrymaster was absent across the Forth so Corbett told his escort to rest; they opened their provisions, ate and drank and then lay on the sand-strewn grass, enjoying the warm noon sun and listening to the birds overhead and the constant chatter of the bees and crickets. Corbett fell into a light sleep and was awakened by Ranulf with the news that the ferrymaster had returned. Corbett went to meet him; at first the fellow refused to go, saying he was tired and wanted to rest. Corbett offered to double the usual fee and they were soon climbing into the skiff and making their way out across the Forth. The ferrymaster eyed Corbett's heavy purse and slyly asked if there was anything else Corbett wished to know. The clerk shook his head. 'Well,' the man replied between gasps as he heaved at the oars, 'there is something I can tell you.' 'What is it?' Corbett asked excitedly. The man grinned. 'Nothing is free, sir, and a man has to work to earn his money.' Corbett dug into his purse and brought out a few coins. 'Then let us see if you have earned it.' The man rested on his oars. 'The ferryman who drowned. The day before the King crossed, early in the morning, he took a Frenchman across the Forth.' 'Is that all?' Corbett asked disappointedly. The man shrugged. 'That is what his widow said,' he replied. 'I thought it was worth something!' Corbett tossed the coins into his lap and the man began rowing once more.

They landed at Inverkeithing and made their way up the cliffs, the summer sun warming their backs, past Aberdour onto Kinghorn Ness, Corbett showing them the place King Alexander III allegedly fell, before going down the path to the royal manor. They found the place in uproar: the courtyard was full of carts piled high with trunks, chests and bundles of clothing. Servants hurried around, to the shrieked orders of officials, and they had to tend to their own horses in the now emptying stables. Corbett told his companions to wait while he searched for the purveyor, Alexander. He found him in a corner of the hall, already half-drunk. He stared blearily at Corbett, his slack mouth half-open. 'Whish, it is Corbett, the English clerk,' he muttered. 'Any more questions?' Corbett smiled tactfully and sat down opposite him. 'Yes,' he replied. 'As a matter of fact I have. Why all the commotion? What is happening?' 'Happening?' Alexander said. 'The Queen is leaving, that's what is happening. The French ships are at sea. They'll be at Leith in a matter of days and then she'll be gone.' He belched loudly. 'Good riddance, I say. Pregnant! She was no more pregnant than I am!' 'Then why did she claim to be?' Corbett enquired. The purveyor wiped his mouth with the dirty hem of his sleeve. 'I don't know. A woman's condition, I've heard it's happened before or,' he leaned across and slyly tapped the side of his pocked red nose, 'maybe it was the French! 'What do you mean?' Corbett snapped. 'Ah,' Alexander replied. 'Maybe the French told her to act pregnant and so lengthen her stay in Scotland!' 'Why should they want that?' Alexander stared at a point above Corbett's head. 'I don't know,' he muttered. 'It's just a thought. That's all!' Corbett paused. 'Tell me?' he asked. 'Did the French envoy arrive here that morning, the day the King died?' Alexander shook his head. 'Are you sure?' Corbett persisted. 'Sometime early in the day?' 'No,' Alexander answered emphatically. 'The only visitor was the messenger who arrived about that time and left a message that the King would be coming to Kinghorn later that day!' 'You are sure?' 'I am certain. The only visitor who came to Kinghorn was Benstede, who came the day before.' 'What did he want?' Corbett snapped. 'How should I know?' the purveyor crossly replied. 'He came with that strange quiet creature, stayed with the Queen for a while and then left.' 'Did the King come to Kinghorn frequently?' 'At first, yes, and he often summoned the Queen to meet him across the Forth, but in the weeks before he died, his visits became less frequent. A man of impetuous passion,' the purveyor drunkenly concluded. 'Is it possible for me to see the Queen now?' Corbett asked. Alexander shook his head. 'No,' he said. 'She will not see anybody today. Perhaps tomorrow,' he looked speculatively at Corbett. 'Perhaps, for a consideration, I might be able to arrange something.' Corbett slipped a silver coin across the table. 'I would be grateful for that.' He nodded at Alexander, rose and returned to Ranulf.

They were able to pay to stay in a small chamber of the manor and bought their meals at the kitchen and buttery. Corbett was worried as the silver Burnell had furnished him with was nearly gone. He had some more coins stitched into his broad leather pouched belt as well as his own money, but he did not wish to use that. When he returned to London it would take months of arguing with some scrupulous clerk of the Exchequer to get it reimbursed. Corbett only hoped the Queen would see him soon. She did not. The next day, and the day after, his requests for an audience met with a blunt refusal and the clerk had to stay and hope for the best. He met Agnes, the brazen lady-in-waiting, whom he had met on his last visit to Kinghorn. She flirted outrageously, promising that she would secure an interview for him with the Queen but she always seemed to fail. Corbett became tired of her constant witticisms and sly innuendoes so she transferred her attention to Ranulf, who was overjoyed to see the tedium of staying in a manor on the Scottish coast so pleasantly broken. They became constant companions and Corbett often found them playing cat's-cradle in some corner or window embrasure.

For his part, Corbett could only fret and decided to draw up a memorandum on what he had learnt so far:

– Why did Benstede visit the Queen?

– Why did the French envoy take a ferry across the Forth but never arrive at Kinghorn?

– Who delivered the message at Kinghorn gate, a letter to the Queen saying the King could be arriving that evening and telling her to instruct the purveyor to have horses at Inverkeithing, particularly his favourite, the white Tamesin? More mysterious, why was such a message delivered hours before the King actually decided to leave for Kinghorn.

– Most importantly, what did Alexander learn at that Council meeting which changed his attitude, sending him on a journey in very dangerous conditions to court a queen he could scarcely be bothered with a few weeks before?

– Why, when the King did not arrive at Kinghorn, did Queen Yolande not send out a search-party? What was the real reason behind Queen Yolande's false pregnancy?

Corbett studied the list wearily. He was making no real progress. Perhaps, he decided, it was time to leave and report his failure to Burnell. He tried once more to see the Queen but her fat, pompous chamberlain rudely announced that Lady Yolande was leaving Scotland and had no wish to discuss anything with anyone. Corbett dejectedly decided to stay a little longer in Kinghorn and then leave. Meanwhile, he asked Ranulf to learn what he could from his new-found paramour though, privately, he believed nothing would come of that. Two more days passed, the Queen sent no invitation so Corbett angrily ordered Ranulf to pack. His servant protested but Corbett was adamant so the young man prepared to leave. Ranulf muttered indignantly against his strange master who dragged him across this wild country so different from the narrow streets of London and so utterly tedious as well. Now, when he had found a pot of honey, Corbett was hurrying him away. Ranulf thought of the Lady Agnes and moaned; she had proved a fiery lover from the time he had first flung her on her back and lifted her lace-trimmed skirts. After that she needed no invitation and, when he was lying exhausted beside her, she would send him into loud peals of laughter with her spicy, tart wit and skill at mimicry, particularly of that rather stuffy English clerk, Hugh Corbett. Ranulf sighed, he would never understand his master. He slowly packed, made sure his companions did likewise and bade an affectionate farewell to Lady Agnes. A week after they arrived at Kinghorn, they were on the road back to Inverkeithing.

Ranulf tried to engage his master in conversation but Corbett was too depressed to respond. 'The Lady Yolande was not worth visiting,' Ranulf said reassuringly. 'Lady Agnes told me, laughing at a virgin pretending to be pregnant!' Corbett stopped his horse and turned to the startled Ranulf. 'You what?' he roared. 'She said what?' Ranulf repeated what he had said. 'Is that correct?' 'Of course,' Ranulf replied bleakly. 'Those were her very words. Why?' 'Never mind.' Corbett dug into his leather pouch. 'Take these gold coins and go, beg your lady to join us at Inverkeithing. If she will not accept the gold, then tell her I will be back with a warrant for her arrest. Now go!' He turned to one of Burnell's messengers. 'Lend him your horse, you can walk.' Corbett continued into Inverkeithing and went straight to the ale-house where he had told Ranulf to meet him. The clerk could scarcely control his excitement, the dull image which had formed in his mind was beginning to take flesh. The shadows were disappearing, something of substance was there. He hired a greasy table and sat, impatiently, waiting for Ranulf to arrive. When he did, with a flustered Lady Agnes in tow, Corbett abruptly told him to leave and asked Agnes to sit on the crude bench opposite him. He poured her a cup of the best wine the dingy house could offer, and leaned forward. 'Lady Agnes, what did you mean by referring to Queen Yolande as a virgin pretending to be pregnant?' The woman's high colour deepened and she fumbled with the cup of wine. 'It was a jest,' she protested. 'A funny story to amuse Ranulf.' 'No, Agnes,' Corbett snapped. 'Do you remember when I met Lady Yolande? She told me she was pregnant or, as she put it, "enceinte". You laughed then. So tell me, or I will arrange for others to take over the questioning.'

Agnes bit her fleshy lower lip and stared anxiously around. 'I suppose it does not matter now the French bitch is leaving. Oh,' she continued softly, 'King Alexander was hot for her but the marriage was never consummated.' 'What!' Corbett exclaimed. 'After five months of marriage?' 'The Lady Yolande first protested she was unwell from the sea voyage, then it was her time of the month when ...' Agnes' voice faltered, 'when a woman's body bleeds. Then she made complaints about the King's mistresses and demanded their total removal from court. The King, she announced, would have to prove his household was cleared of these doxies before she allowed him into her bed. In the weeks before His Grace's sudden death, it was just excuses, a total refusal to consummate the marriage.' 'How do you know this? You were scarce close confidantes. I noticed that on my first visit to Kinghorn.' Agnes nodded. 'I hated the spoilt bitch. King Alexander ordered me into her retinue; I got bored and used to listen to her conversations with the one French lady-in-waiting she brought with her, a girl called Marie. They thought I could not understand French; I can, my mother was French. That is why I was put in her household. I am fluent in the tongue. I fully understood what she was saying to you the day you visited Kinghorn, which is why I almost burst out laughing.' 'For what reason?' enquired Corbett. 'Do you think Yolande refused to consummate the marriage?' Agnes shrugged. 'I have heard of similar cases. Young girls frightened of the pain the act causes. Nunneries are full of them.' She laughed at her own joke. 'Yolande could well have been terrified of Alexander, or,' she added, 'Yolande may have been a lover of other women. When I watched her and the girl Marie I sometimes wondered. The King,' she added thoughtfully, almost to herself, 'could have forced her but that was not Alexander's way. He never forced a woman in his life. I also believe he genuinely loved her.' 'That is all you can tell me?' Corbett asked. 'That,' said Lady Agnes, rising to her feet, 'is all I can tell you because that is all I know. I would be grateful if you would let Ranulf escort me back to Kinghorn.' Corbett nodded and Lady Agnes swept out of the room.

The clerk waited till Ranulf returned and, when he did, they all made their way down to the ferry and across the Forth. The ferrymaster regaled them with spicy stories about the comings and goings of King Alexander. Ranulf laughed and baited him, Corbett heard him out until they had reached the jetty at Dalmeny. 'Tell me,' he said, 'the other ferryman, you said he had a widow. Where does she live?' The ferryman pointed to a thatched, low-roofed timbered hut further along the shoreline. 'You'll find her there, poor woman. Joan Taggart. Her husband only received the letters patent from the King to act as ferryman just before his death.'

Corbett nodded; he told Ranulf to collect and saddle their horses while he walked down to Joan Taggart's house. A small, brown-haired woman met him at the door, surrounded by a group of noisy, dirty children who eyed Corbett boldly, then ran to hide and giggle behind their mother's skirts. Corbett bowed. 'Joan Taggart?' he said. 'Aye.' 'I am Hugh Corbett, clerk. I wish to talk to you about your husband's death. I do not wish to upset you.' The woman just stared at him. 'Do you speak English?' 'I am English,' the woman replied abruptly. 'I come from the border lands. What do you want with my husband's death?' 'He died the same night as the King?' Corbett asked. 'He didn't die,' replied Joan, 'he was murdered, but no one believes me.' She turned and shooed the flock of children away. 'Nobody believes me,' she continued, 'but my husband was a sailor, he knew the water.' She squinted up at the sun. 'A Frenchman, I don't know who, was using him. The same day the King died, late in the morning, this mysterious Frenchman hired my husband's boat and services to take him across to Inverkeithing. My husband came back excited and said he would be going out again late in the evening. The storm came up and burst on the Forth. I begged my husband to stay but he was excited. He said the Frenchman would pay generously.' 'And then what?' Corbett asked. 'He left.' The woman stopped speaking, blinked back the tears from her eyes and swallowed before continuing. 'The next morning, he was found, head down, bobbing like some stupid cork in the shallow water.' 'And his boat?' Corbett queried. 'Still tied up,' the woman replied. 'The coroner came and said my husband must have been drunk, fell and drowned. After all, there was no mark on the body.' 'So, what makes you think it was murder?' Corbett persisted with his questioning. Joan pushed the greying hair from her brow. 'At first,' she replied slowly, 'I accepted it was an accident but then later, when it was too late to do anything about it, I remembered the way the boat had been tied up.' She looked directly at Corbett. 'Every sailor has his own way of tying a knot. My husband's boat was beached and tied but he never fastened that knot. I believe he went out that night with the Frenchman, whoever he is, and crossed the Forth. When he returned, he was murdered. His boat beached and tied up by other hands, probably the same ones which murdered him.' Corbett stared past her at the timbered house. 'You are sure,' he questioned, 'that it was a Frenchman?' 'Yes, my husband called him that. Why, do you know him?' Corbett thought of de Craon's evil smirk and then Bruce with his cruel mouth and perfect knowledge of French. 'No, Madam,' he lied. 'I know no one of that nationality. But why do you not tell the authorities, petition the Council?' Joan shrugged. 'And who would believe me?' 'True, Madam! True!' Corbett muttered, bowed and was about to turn away when the woman caught his arm. 'Sir!' she exclaimed. 'My children and I now starve!' Corbett looked into her harassed face and fearful eyes and, digging into his purse, drew out some coins and handed them to her. 'Thank you,' he said. 'Perhaps I can do more! I will see what I can do.'

Corbett strode back to where Ranulf and his companions sat with the horses. 'Make yourselves comfortable here,' he snapped. 'I intend to return across the Forth. 'Tis a minor matter,' he continued, ignoring Ranulf's groan, 'but there is something I must find.' He then went down the slope to where the ferrymaster was preparing to beach his craft. 'I wish to return,' Corbett said. The man shrugged. 'It will cost you.' 'Yes, I know,' answered Corbett testily. 'But this time I want to land, not at Inverkeithing but,' he stared across the water, 'at some secret place far from public view where I could stable a horse without arousing suspicion or interest.' The ferryman nodded. 'Yes, I know of such a place, but it is going to cost you even more. You had best get in.' They both clambered aboard and the man pulled the boat out into the main current. As he rowed, the man explained. 'There are,' he said, 'caves up from the beach, just across the Forth to the west of Inverkeithing. I will take you there.'

The man was true to his word. They landed on a sandy, gravel beach; above them rose cliffs which ran along the entire coast. The ferryman indicated with a wave of his hand. 'If you go up there,' he said, 'you will see them. They are like small chambers; they were once used by pirates, only His Grace, the late King, cleared them out with fire, sword, and gallows. Do you wish me to stay?' 'Yes,' Corbett said. 'If I am not successful in finding what I am looking for I shall return and tell you.'

Corbett slipped another coin into the man's hand and,

while the ferryman made himself comfortable in the shadow of his boat, Corbett began the long arduous climb up the hill. Soon he reached the top where the hills levelled out and stretched to the hard rock face of the towering cliffs. He immediately saw what the ferrymaster had been talking about. At the base of these cliffs, almost as if they had been hewn in the rock by men, were three, four or five cave-mouths, chamber-like, as if they were a row of monastic cells in some monastery. Corbett made his way through the thick clogged sand and entered the first one. There were signs of human habitation, scraps of litter, faint smells, broken pottery, strange markings on the walls of the caves which seemed to stretch for ever down into the blackness beneath the cliffs. Corbett's heart sank when he noticed this. If all the chambers were as long as this, or if they were only used by people who had gone down deep into them, then his search would take months. He decided to go on to the second and third caves, determined to find what he was looking for. In the fourth cavern he did. Just within the entrance there were mounds of horse dung. He picked some up in his hand and crumbled it. Corbett reckoned horses had been stabled there within the last two or three months. There were other signs, a ragged, empty bag bearing traces of oats and a clump of dark wet material which, Corbett realised, was once hay. Satisfied, he knelt and cleansed his hands in a pool of salt water and walked back down to where the ferryman was patiently waiting for him.

FOURTEEN

After recrossing the Forth, Corbett joined his party. Their journey back began uneventfully. They crossed Dalmeny bridge and were in open countryside when the attackers struck. Five or six men, horsed, masked and well-armed, burst from a clump of trees and bore down on them. Corbett grabbed the crossbow, already loaded, which swung from his saddlebow and brought it up, aimed and sent the quarrel deep into the chest of the leading rider. Then the rest were amongst them, slashing with short-sword, mace and club. Ranulf and his companions drew their swords and cut, thrust and screamed at their assailants. Corbett whirled his big Welsh dagger, dug his spurs in and, shouting at the rest to follow him, broke through and galloped from the trees where the ambush had taken place. It was a tactic Corbett had seen used in Wales, cavalry never stopping to confront an enemy but breaking away, eluding the trap. Corbett saw two of the assailants go down screaming, clutching red spouting wounds and hoped the rest would be too chastened to follow, surprised by the fierce resistance they had encountered.

After a while, Corbett called a halt; his horse was half-blown and he realised there was no sign of any pursuit. He was unscathed but almost sick with fear.

Ranulf had bruises and cuts on his hands, arms and legs but one of the others, a young man, had received a terrible slash across his stomach and Corbett knew the fellow would be dead very soon. The blood poured out from the gash while he groaned and begged for water. Corbett gave it to him, knowing it might hasten his end. They took him from his horse, and laid him tenderly on the ground; Ranulf stood watch while they waited quietly for the man to die. He did, on a frothy gurgle of blood. Corbett said the "Miserere" and "Requiem" realising he did not even know the man's name. Someone's brother, baby son, or lover he thought and now he was gone: Corbett looked down at the corpse and felt the futility of the death. He ordered a cloak to be draped and tied round the body which was then slung over a horse and they continued on their way to the Abbey of Holy Rood. They reached it late at night, Corbett fearful of every shadow and ill to the point of nausea with exhaustion and tension. He brushed the sleepy Prior's enquiries aside, asked him to take care of the body, promising he would meet any expense. Then he and Ranulf trudged wearily off to bed.

Next morning they attended the Requiem Mass for their dead colleague who had been dressed by the monks for burial and now lay in a new pine coffin in front of the sanctuary steps of the abbey church. The Prior, resplendent in black and gold vestments, stood arms outstretched, and intoned the Introit: 'Requiem aeternam. Dona ei Domine. Eternal rest grant unto him, O Lord, and let perpetual light shine upon him.' Corbett rubbed his eyes wearily and wondered when he would rest from this interminable business, who the attackers of yesterday were and, more importantly, who had paid them? The choir intoned the sequence, the beautiful poem of Thomas di Celano, "Dies Irae, Dies Illa":

O, day of wrath, O day of mourning
See fulfilled the Prophet's warning,
Heaven and Earth in ashes burning.

Corbett caught phrases, "See from Heaven the Judge descendeth" and, turning to look at the coffin, vowed that the young man awaiting burial would not have to wait until Judgement Day for justice.

After the burial, Corbett sent the equally frightened Ranulf off to the castle, reassuring him that all would be well and authorising him to seek an audience with Bishop Wishart. He was to ask the good bishop to grant Corbett an interview and to have the late King's confessor present as well. Corbett added that he would appreciate an armed escort to the castle and so required the company of Sir James Selkirk and others of his ilk. Late in the afternoon, Ranulf returned with Sir James and a small convoy of cavalry and, without further ado, Corbett saddled a horse and rode back with them to the castle. Sir James attempted to exchange light bantering talk, asking Corbett if he wanted to experience his hospitality once again. When Corbett replied that Sir James's hospitality was equal to his manners, the knight lapsed into a sullen silence.

At the castle, Corbett was immediately taken to the Bishop's chamber. Wishart was waiting for him, sitting behind his long, polished table almost as if he had not moved since Corbett saw him last. Beside the Bishop was a tall, thin, ascetic man, wearing the black and brown garb of a Franciscan monk who Corbett immediately assumed was Father John.

'Come in, English Clerk,' the Bishop beckoned Corbett and Ranulf to the bench before his table. 'Tell us why the impetuous command? What is the urgency?' 'My Lord,' Corbett replied, not bothering to sit down, 'I would like to ask Father John, and I presume this is he, why His Grace, the late King, was sending him to Rome?' The monk licked his lips and looked sideways at the Bishop. 'My Lord,' he muttered. 'I cannot, I was told "sub sigillo", under the seal of confession. I cannot tell anyone. Not even the Holy Father can command me to do that!'

The Bishop pursed his lips, nodded and looked expectantly at Corbett. 'Father,' Corbett replied. 'I know canon law and I also know that it rests on the justice of God. I do not wish you to violate your oath of secrecy or your conscience but,' and he turned to look eagerly at the Bishop, 'with His Lordship's permission, I would like to take you aside and quietly ask you one question? If I am wrong, you may say nothing, and I vow I will not ask you again.' The Bishop turned to the Franciscan who swallowed nervously and nodded his assent. The Bishop looked at Corbett with raised eyebrows and gestured to him to proceed. Ranulf watched his master and the friar go over to the far side of the room. Corbett whispered a few words and the friar looked up sharply and nodded. 'Sic habes,' he said, quoting the Latin tag. 'You have it!' Corbett smiled and walked back to sit down on the stool while Father John bowed to Wishart and silently left the room.

The Bishop stared quizzically at Corbett. 'What was it he said to you?' he asked. 'For the time being, my Lord, I prefer to stay silent on the matter. But tell me, my Lord, the circumstances of Erceldoun's death?' The Bishop fumbled amongst the pieces of parchment which littered his table and, leaning over the table, threw one scroll into Corbett's lap. 'The Coroner's report. You may read it.' Corbett studied the scrawled report of Matthew Relston, Coroner, "taken in June 1286 on the body of Thomas Erceldoun found in the chancel of St. Giles Church on the evening of 26th June by parishioners of the said church. His body bore no sign of violence except for a weal around his neck. An investigation into the events leading up to his death revealed that Erceldoun had told people he was going down to St. Giles Church to meet a priest. Who the latter was is difficult to establish. The verdict is that Erceldoun was murdered by person or persons unknown".

Corbett handed the scroll back to the Bishop. 'That is all?' he asked. 'Yes,' replied Wishart. 'I doubt if he intended to meet a priest or that Erceldoun was murdered by one; he was a powerfully-built young soldier, I doubt very much if any priest, or even more than one, could get the advantage of such a man.' 'I would like to examine his corpse,' Corbett said. 'Impossible!' Wishart snapped. 'I must!' Corbett replied firmly. 'And not only his, but Seton's as well!' He heard Ranulf groan beside him. 'You, my Lord Bishop, can give permission. It could be done late at night with no dishonour for the men's relations or lack of respect.' 'It is essential, you say?' 'It is, my Lord. I also need the protection of Sir James Selkirk.' 'Against whom?' the Bishop barked. 'I don't know, my Lord, but the waters I am wading through are deep, murky and treacherous.' He looked straight into Wishart's hooded eyes. 'For all I know, it could be you that I must be wary of!' Wishart stared at Corbett and laughed as if Corbett had told some pleasantry. He then wrote, his quill pen scratching a piece of vellum. He finished, sanded what he had written, waxed and sealed it, then gave it to Corbett. 'Your warrant, English Clerk. Do what you have to do and do it quickly!' He looked at Selkirk. 'Tonight, you must carry out the business.' He nodded at Corbett. 'For the moment, farewell, but remember I will ask you to give an account of your stewardship here.'

Corbett stayed in the castle the rest of the day,

wandering about, looking for any place he could sit and quietly meditate on all he knew. The picture forming in his mind was clearer, more distinct, though he could scarce believe it. Wandering aimlessly down one of the grim, draughty passageways of the castle, with Ranulf trailing behind him like some morose dog, Corbett almost bumped into Benstede and his strange body-servant, Aaron. 'Master Corbett!' Benstede exclaimed, his round, plump face wreathed in smiles. 'At last! I heard of your problems with Selkirk. Of course, I immediately protested to the Council. You have also been attacked, I hear?' Corbett nodded. 'At least twice, the last time on our way into Edinburgh. A member of Bishop Burnell's household was killed!' Benstede looked grimly around. 'The same is true of me. Two or three weeks ago, a crossbow quarrel narrowly missed my face as we crossed the Lawnmarket. I suspected de Craon. He has been plotting since his arrival in Scotland. He was constantly closeted with the late King. Even the day before the King died! I understood from the expression on his face when the meeting was over, that the encounter with the King was not a pleasant one.' Corbett shrugged. 'Then we must all be on our guard!' he commented. 'Is there news from England?' Benstede sighed. 'None. Burnell and his entourage are coming north. King Edward is still in France.' He squeezed Corbett's arm, 'Take care, Master Clerk,' and continued on his way, his servant padding behind him like some silent dark shadow.

Corbett watched them go and smiled to himself at what he had learnt. So, Burnell was coming north. Good! There was every chance that he and Ranulf would be ordered to leave Scotland to join him.

Late that evening, Corbett was found by a servant sent by Selkirk, who announced in broad Scots that the knight would be grateful if Corbett joined him in the outer bailey near the main gate. Corbett and Ranulf finished off the meagre scraps of food they had begged from the kitchen and hurried down. Selkirk and four soldiers, well-armed, carrying picks and shovels, were waiting rather self-consciously near the main gate.

Corbett smiled. 'If you are ready, Sir James? The bodies are buried where?' 'The graveyard of St. Giles,' Sir James testily remarked, looking up into the night sky. 'There is a full moon, so we will not need torches. I have already discovered where the graves lie. So, come, let's be done with it!' They walked down into the town, now concealed by darkness, despite regulations that lantern horns were to be displayed outside each house. A curfew had been imposed, explained Selkirk, because of the situation following the King's death. Most law-abiding citizens obeyed it but not so the denizens of the slums, stinking alleys and runnels of Edinburgh. Time and again Corbett saw shadows flit across their path, heard movement in the darkness which fell quiet as they approached. In the main, they were alone, their boots ringing hollow on the hard enclosed tracks except for the scavenging cat and threatening rustle of rats gnawing in the heaps of refuse which littered every street. They entered the Lawnmarket and Corbett shivered when he saw the gibbet and its rotten, swaying human fruit, black figures against the moonlit, summer night sky. The huge mass of St. Giles rose above them. They entered the enclosure and walked down the side of the church into the dark, tree-filled cemetery beyond. Here, they stopped, the soldiers trying to hide their fear and Corbett sensed that even Sir James Selkirk was frightened to be there. The dead, Corbett thought, do not worry me, it is the living who plot and kill.

'You can take us to the graves, Sir James?' Selkirk

nodded. 'It is strange,' continued Corbett, 'that Erceldoun is buried in the very church in which he was murdered!' Sir James disagreed. 'Both Erceldoun and Seton died in early summer,' he pointed out. 'Both men came from humble backgrounds, their kin could not afford to transport the bodies home, so they were brought here. Which grave do you wish to see first?' 'Erceldoun's,' snapped Corbett. Sir James led his group through a small wicket-gate and across the long, soft grass. The silence was oppressive as they made their way past mounds of earth, some with battered wooden crosses, others just forlorn heaps of clay. The rich could afford stone memorials, exquisitely carved, but the graves of the poor were not even properly dug, shallow holes which scarcely concealed their dead, left open to scavenging dogs and other creatures. Time and again, they came upon heaps of white shard-like bones or tripped cursing over a trailing white, skeletal arm or leg protruding from its thin veil of soil.

An owl-hoot startled them all and a soldier cursed as the bird sailed low over their heads, plunging in the grass to seize some little creature which squirmed in its death agonies. 'Come!' said Selkirk impatiently. They walked a little further. Selkirk looked round and pointed to fresh-cut grass which surrounded a mound of newly-dug soil. 'Erceldoun's grave,' he remarked and after lighting a cresset-torch with a tinder flint ordered the soldiers to start digging. It was an easy task, the grave was shallow and soon they had scraped the dirt off the still-white coffin lid. 'Open it!' ordered Corbett but the soldier simply shook his head, threw his spade down and walked away. Corbett dug out his long Welsh dagger, knelt down beside the grave and prised open the lid. It scraped and creaked but eventually broke free. Corbett gagged at the bitter-sweet smell of corruption and covered his mouth and nose with his cloak to prevent himself choking. In the light of Selkirk's flickering torch the corpse lay face up, the head slightly askew, the eyes half-open. Putrefaction had set in around the nose and mouth, the skin felt cold and soggy as Corbett gently turned the head to look at the fatal weal round the neck, a broad, purple black gash with little round indentations which made it look like some ghostly parody of a necklace.

Corbett looked down at the fearful remains of a young man who, the last time they had met, had been a vigorous young soldier interested in clearing his own name. Now he was dead, brutally murdered, and Corbett knew his only crime was that someone had watched them talk. He wiped his hands on the wet grass beside the grave and ordered the reluctant soldier back to secure the lid of the coffin and cover it with soil. Corbett noticed that the escort was no longer round him. Ranulf was sitting yards away and the soldiers were crowded together muttering and cursing to each other whilst Selkirk had already moved across the cemetery to a nearby grave. 'If you have finished there,' Sir James called out softly. 'This is Seton's grave.' Again the soldiers scraped away the dirt and Corbett prised open the wooden lid. He rolled back the leather covering and heard Selkirk's gasp of surprise. The young man lying there was short of stature, blond, and though he had been in the ground much longer than Erceldoun the body, though swollen and green-tinged, had hardly begun to decompose. 'By the Hand of God!' Selkirk muttered. 'How has a body which has been in the ground remained so fresh?' 'I do not know,' answered Corbett. 'But I have my suspicions. I am not surprised. I almost expected to find it so.' Seton's body was quickly reinterred and, despite Sir James' protests, Corbett insisted that his escort accompany him back to the Abbey of Holy Rood. They returned without incident. Corbett curtly thanked Sir James, wished him goodnight and, followed by a relieved Ranulf, gratefully entered the cool darkness of the abbey buildings.

FIFTEEN

The following day Corbett was busy in the abbey scriptorium, seated at a small desk, writing out a list of facts, snorting with fury at his own mistakes which he would angrily cross out with a score of his pen and begin again. Ranulf came in with a series of plaintive questions but Corbett dismissed him with a look. The Prior, ever curious, also tried to intervene but Corbett, taciturn and withdrawn, made it plain he did not want to answer questions. Once this list was completed and each point neatly itemised, Corbett picked it up, left the sweet, fragrant-smelling library to walk slowly round the cloisters, muttering to himself, referring now and again to the piece of parchment held tightly in his hand, like some preacher learning his words, or a student preparing to discuss his treatise. The monks, unused to such curious behaviour, gossiped with relish about the strange eccentricities of this English clerk. Corbett did not mind; he broke off his constant walking for a meal of fish broiled in milk and herbs, then returned to his task. The images so vague in his mind were now quite clear and distinct but he had to be certain: the solution must be presented like a concise clear legal document, everything in its right place and, unfortunately, there were still gaps to be filled and ragged ends tidied up.

Late in the afternoon, he asked and obtained from the now bemused Prior the services of the lay brother who had accompanied them to Earlston. Ranulf was ordered to saddle the horses and Corbett led his little party from the abbey and up into the town. He was pleased to see that as soon as they left the abbey gate, they were joined by the soldiers Sir James Selkirk had stationed near the abbey. Corbett was oblivious to everything else as he travelled down into the city: the dirty streets, the noisy clamour of the traders, even the mixture of rich smells from bakeries, cookshops and heaps of human and animal ordure steaming in the summer sun. He was trying to remember the route he had taken the morning de Craon's men had stopped him. The heat in the narrow packed streets was stifling and Sir James' men began to complain loudly; the lay brother, used to Corbett's strange ways, slumped resignedly on his gentle cob whilst Ranulf looked askance at his erratic and peculiar master.

At last, Corbett found the narrow alleyway and pushed his horse through the crowd to the battered ale-stake above the dingy house. Ranulf and the escort were told to wait outside but the lay brother was asked to come in for he could, as Corbett put it, "talk in the common language". Ranulf, outside, peered through the small window, its shabby wooden shutters flung wide to let in the air and light. The place was just like any ale-house or tavern in Southwark with its dirt-beaten floor and ramshackle tables, filled with traders and peasants eager to spend the profits of market day. Ranulf watched Corbett, the lay brother acting as interpreter, in deep conversation with the tavern-keeper. After a while, Corbett nodded, handed over a few coins and left, his face wreathed in a complacent smile.

They made their way back, not to the abbey but the castle, Corbett sending ahead one of his escort to ask

Wishart for an audience and when they arrived the old, foxy-faced Bishop was waiting for them in his now sweltering chambers, though still swathed in fur-trimmed robes. 'The blood thins, Master Clerk,' he apologised. 'I go to meet my death. One day, perhaps sooner than you think, you might meet yours!' Corbett ignored the hidden threat and relaxed in the chair the servant had brought him. Apart from Selkirk, they were alone, for Corbett had left Ranulf and the escort to relax and refresh themselves.

'You wanted to see me, Master Clerk, so come to the point!' Corbett sensed the Bishop was tense, anxious, even frightened. 'My Lord,' he said. 'Did the late King ever discuss his marriage with you?' 'No,' the Bishop was emphatic. 'His Highness was, er, loath to discuss such matters with me.' 'With anyone then?' 'Not to my knowledge. The King kept personal matters to himself.' 'Were the French envoys an exception, particularly in the days preceding his death?' Corbett persisted with his questioning. 'Yes,' the Bishop replied slowly, trying to create time to think. 'But this is not an English trial, Master Corbett. So, why the pert questions? Am I before a court?' 'My Lord,' Corbett genuinely apologised. 'I did not intend to give offence but I can see an end to this matter. I will inform you of it but I am impatient.' Corbett paused before continuing. 'Well, were the French envoys privy to the King's secrets?' The Bishop picked up a long thin parchment-knife and balanced it in a vein-streaked, brown-spotted hand. 'Alexander was a good king,' he replied cautiously. 'He kept Scotland peaceful, but, as a man, he was ruled by his codpiece. When his children died, he dallied, did not enter into a marriage contract but then agreed to marry the Princess Yolande. At first, matters went well. The kingdom hoped for an heir but the King became surly, angry and withdrawn; he shunned the

French envoys but, yes, in the days preceding, even the day before his death, he was closeted with them.'

Wishart squirmed in his seat, angry and impatient at the impertinent questions of this English clerk. He would have liked to order him from the kingdom, send him trussed across the border with a curt note to his arrogant king. The Bishop looked at the white, lean-faced clerk. There were many things he would have liked to have done but he needed this man, who, with a combination of chance and logic, could reach the truths which might affect the realm.

Wishart leaned forward and fished amongst the pieces of parchment on his table, took up a thin scroll and tossed it to Corbett. 'You asked for this,' he commented, 'or rather the man you sent demanding an audience asked for it.' Corbett nodded muttering his thanks and carefully unrolled it. The parchment was merely a list drawn up in a clerkly hand describing the effects and property of one "Patrick Seton Esquire". Corbett studied the list intently, grunted with pleasure, handed it back to Wishart and rose. 'My Lord,' he said, 'thank you for your time and assistance. I would like to ask one more question of Sir James Selkirk?' Wishart shrugged. 'Ask it!' he replied. 'I believe,' began Corbett, turning to Selkirk, 'that you were sent by Bishop Wishart early on the morning of 19th March to ensure that all was well with the King. You took the ferry at Dalmeny and then used the horses from the royal stables at Aberdour to journey to Kinghorn, and it was then you found the King's body lying on the beach?' The knight grunted. 'Yes,' he replied. 'That is what happened. There is nothing extraordinary in that, is there?' 'Oh, but there is,' Corbett said smoothly. 'Was it common practice for you to journey after the King to ensure all was well. And, if you were riding along the cliffs at Kinghorn, how on earth did you see the King's corpse lying on the rocks below?' Selkirk grasped Corbett hard by the wrist. 'I do not like you, English Clerk,' he muttered menacingly. 'I do not like your arrogance and your questions, and if I had my way I would arrange an accident or have you thrown into some deep dungeon until everyone had forgotten about you!' 'Selkirk,' Wishart snapped. 'You forget yourself! You know there is an answer to the clerk's questions, so why not give it!' Selkirk released his grip on Corbett and fell back in his chair. 'It was common practice,' he commented, 'for Alexander III to ride like a demon around his kingdom. This was not the first time and, if he had survived, certainly would not have been the last. The King was constantly on the move. It was almost as if there was a devil inside him. He could not rest. His Grace the Bishop,' he nodded towards his patron, 'often sent me after the King to ensure that all was well. On a number of occasions I found members of the royal household resting. Their horses blown and they themselves suffering some injury. I expected no different when his Lordship sent me out on the morning of the 19th. Accompanied by two men-at-arms, I crossed the Forth at Dalmeny and took horses from the royal stable at Aberdour. You know little about Scotland, Master Corbett, or about the sea. By the time we crossed the Forth, it was early morning, the tide was out, so we did not take the cliff-top path but rode along the beach. The storm had petered out, it was a good morning and our horses were fresh. We galloped along the sand, and I knew what had happened long before we reached the rocks where the King lay. I saw the white of Tamesin, the dead King's horse, as well as Alexander's purple cloak blowing in the wind. The King was lying amongst the rocks and it was apparent he was dead. He had fallen between two sharp jagged-edge boulders and the angry tide had battered his body between them. His face was a mass of wounds, his neck completely broken. If it had not been for his clothes and the rings on his fingers I would have scarcely recognised him.' 'And the horse?' Corbett queried. 'Not worth looking at,' Selkirk replied. 'Again, a mass of wounds, two of its legs broken, the head fully twisted round. We removed the harness from the horse and made a rough bier for the King's corpse. After which we returned to Aberdour where a royal barge later brought the King's body across the Firth of Forth.' 'So,' Corbett enquired, 'you never went along to Kinghorn Ness or examined the place where the King may have fallen?' 'No,' Selkirk replied slowly. 'Though we knew by the place where he had fallen that it must have been at the very summit just as the path runs down the cliff to Kinghorn Manor.' Corbett smiled tactfully. 'Then I owe you the most sincere apologies, Sir James,' he commented. 'I always thought you went along Kinghorn Ness and found the body below you and then had it raised by ropes.' Selkirk snorted with laughter. 'Why should I do that? I have already told you that the tide was out. Any traveller would have taken the same route as I did. You only use the path along the cliff in bad weather or if there is a possibility you might be trapped by the tide. But your question about ropes and tackle lifting the body is pure nonsense, man!'

Corbett nodded his acceptance. 'There is one further favour, your Lordship,' Corbett said slowly. 'But it needs to be done, even though it may give offence to the French.' 'Go on,' said Wishart wearily. 'I have been to Kinghorn Manor,' Corbett continued. 'I have attempted to see Queen Yolande to ask her why she did not send out a search-party for the King when he failed to arrive at Kinghorn Manor. I find it strange that a wife, a queen, a princess with responsibilities, who had been informed in no uncertain fashion that her husband was to join her, fails to do anything when he does not arrive. Any woman with commonsense would immediately become alarmed and send out some of her household to find the King. After all, he could have been thrown from his horse and been lying injured on the moors in the middle of a fierce storm. I must ask Queen Yolande why she acted as she did.' Corbett watched the old Bishop carefully. On the one hand he saw his own suspicions mirrored in the Bishop's eyes, on the other Wishart realised that such an interview might alienate the French and cause more trouble than it was worth. Corbett decided to press the point. 'For all we know, your Lordship, it is possible that Queen Yolande was involved in her husband's death. For her sake, for France's sake, for Scotland's sake, such suspicions must be cleared!' Wishart nodded slowly. 'Queen Yolande,' he replied, 'is to leave on tomorrow's tide just after dawn. A French galley will pick her up off the coast of the Forth and take her out to the sea where other ships are waiting to escort her back to France. I understand that the French envoy, de Craon, will be seeing her off.' The Bishop heaved a sigh. 'If the French ship leaves the Forth,' he continued, 'there is little chance that they will stop to answer your questions, Master Clerk. So you must stop her before her ship leaves the Forth.' The Bishop suddenly stirred himself. 'Do we have a ship, Sir James?' the Bishop asked. 'Of course,' Selkirk replied. 'I mean,' the Bishop retorted brusquely, 'is there a ship in the port of Leith we can use?' Selkirk rubbed his mouth with his hand. 'There is the "St. Andrew",' he said, 'a cog we often use to protect our ships from English pirates.' He looked sideways at Corbett. 'It has a full complement, a crew, an armoury and is good for putting to sea at a moment's notice.' 'Ah well,' Wishart smiled. 'Sir James, take our English visitor to the port of Leith and order the captain to follow his directions across the Forth. He is to stop the ship, speak to Queen Yolande and not allow her to leave the Firth of Forth until Corbett has satisfactory answers to questions which intrigue even me. I will give you the necessary warrants and letters.'

SIXTEEN

Within an hour Corbett and Selkirk, accompanied by a dozen mounted men-at-arms, were pounding along the muddy track which led from Edinburgh to the port of Leith. Their progress was fast, the ground had hardened after the rains while Sir James had unfurled the royal standard of Scotland to make it obvious to any others using the road to stand aside quickly and let them pass. They galloped into Leith, up its narrow winding streets, across the cobbled market-place where Corbett had met Bruce's retainers, and then down to the quayside. There was a mass of shipping in the port, small skiffs, boats, the huge heavy-bottomed sterns of Hanseatic merchantmen. Small cranes were dragging out or depositing bales, barrels, chests and huge leather bags. There was a confusion of sounds, strange oaths, cries and orders, while ships arrived or prepared to depart. Sir James paid no heed, leading his small party along the quayside, ordering people aside and ignoring the oaths and catcalls which followed them.

Eventually they found the "Saint Andrew", a large warlike craft with a bluff tub-like hull. The body of the ship rose high above the quay, its stern crowned by small castles or crenellated fighting-platforms to protect archers and soldiers during battle. The huge single mast had its large sail furled under the platform used by the look-out.

Sir James hailed the ship, telling the crew they were coming aboard and a large gangplank was lowered. Sir James ordered one of his retinue to stay and stable the horses while he and Corbett, accompanied by the remainder of his party, made their way carefully up the gangplank and into the busy ship. The crew moved about jostling each other; Corbett gathered that the ship had recently returned to port and the crew were busily cleaning the decks. He saw a vast patch of blood and guessed that the ship must have been in one of the many petty skirmishes which took place at sea, for ships of various nations, Norway, Denmark, England, Scotland and France used these waters for fishing, trade and piracy.

A young, red-haired man, dressed simply in a leather jerkin, leggings and boots, came up to Corbett and spoke in an accent the English clerk could not even hope to follow. Selkirk, however, made himself clearly understood. The man, curious, looked narrowly at Corbett and was about to refuse until Selkirk showed him Wishart's sealed warrant. The captain, for Corbett guessed it must be he, let out a litany of rich oaths in a variety of languages leaving Corbett in no doubt about his feelings concerning the mission. Nevertheless, the fellow began to bark orders. The decks were cleared; sailors began to run like monkeys up the rigging unfurling the great sail, while two more were sent up to the stern-castle to manage the huge tiller. After a while the captain, much calmer, took Selkirk and Corbett down to his cabin under the fo'castle, a small, dingy room smelling of tar and salt, and containing a simple cot bed, trunk, table and a number of stools. Corbett, unused to the gentle rocking of the ship and the low beams, banged his head as he straightened up. The pain was intense and though the captain laughed at his discomfort, he offered Corbett a cup of surprisingly good wine to ease the pain and, as Selkirk put it, strengthen his stomach for the coming voyage.

Within an hour of embarkation, the "Saint Andrew" had turned and was making its way across the Firth. The pain in Corbett's head subsided only to be replaced by a growing sense of nausea as the ship rocked and rolled on the water. Selkirk sat enjoying the English clerk's discomfort. 'Come, Master Corbett,' he said jovially. 'You had best come up on deck if you are to be sick. You cannot vomit here and upset our host. Moreover, he will need direction.' Corbett muttered curses but followed Selkirk up the ladder and on to the deck of the ship. The large sail, now unfurled, was billowing in the strong wind as the ship circled across the water towards the far-distant shoreline. The Firth was much broader here than at Dalmeny and, if it had not been a clear day, Corbett could have almost believed they were out on the open sea. The captain showed them a rough map drawn crudely on tough, brown vellum and with a stubby finger and guttural comments pointed out the coastline of Fife, the manor of Kinghorn and the possible place where the French could dock to pick up a party from the beach. 'What is he saying?' Corbett asked. Selkirk shrugged. 'There is no port at Kinghorn but there are a number of fishing villages and coves along the coast where Queen Yolande would go to wait for the ship. It is a question of simply following the coast down until we actually catch sight of the ship itself.' Selkirk looked up at the darkening sky. 'It will soon be night,' he commented, 'and we won't be able to see anything. The captain has promised to reach the coastline by early dawn and follow it down to the sea. It is our only hope.' Selkirk talked to the captain for a while in a language which he later explained was Erse, the tongue of the Isles, before taking Corbett back to the cabin.

Corbett then spent what must have been one of the most miserable nights he had ever experienced. The captain gave him a bowl of cold stew which he could only swallow by gulping it down with wine. Selkirk threw him a cloak, telling the clerk to make himself as comfortable as possible and Corbett slept fitfully, waking once or twice to go up on deck to vomit his dinner into the sea amidst the jeering catcalls of the night watch. Eventually Corbett decided to stay there, leaning against the rail, watching the day break above him. The captain was true to his word. The ship reached the coastline just after sunrise and began to follow it in a south-easterly direction down to the sea. Their task was not as difficult as Corbett had thought. The crew hailed a fishing-skiff who gave them information that a French ship had been seen making its way up the Firth the previous day. After that, it was simply a matter of having a strong wind, the sailors climbing up and down the rigging, adjusting the sail to catch every breeze and puff of air while look-outs were posted high above the mast.

The ship settled down to a monotonous routine until the cries of the look-outs brought Selkirk and the captain back onto the deck. The "Saint Andrew" nosed by a headland and into a small cove where a large two-masted galley was preparing to make sail. 'What shall we do now?' Corbett asked. 'Stop it!' Selkirk replied tersely. He ordered the captain to display the royal standard on the stern, just in case the French believed they were pirates, as the "Saint Andrew" began to run down alongside the galley. Selkirk, stationing himself on the fo'castle, hailed the ship in Scottish and French. At first he was greeted by shouts and catcalls and Corbett wondered if the galley would refuse to heave-to and continue in its dash for the open sea. He joined Selkirk on the poop and watched the figures on the French ship scurrying backwards and forwards on deck.

'De Craon is there,' Selkirk rasped and pointed to a figure at the centre of the galley just between the two masts. The two craft were now alongside, only yards apart on the bobbing water; the Scottish ship had loosened its sail while the oars of the galley were now clear of the sea. Selkirk hailed the French envoy by name, a more civilised conversation ensued, and the "Saint Andrew" was allowed to come alongside. Corbett and Selkirk, accompanied by four men-at-arms, clambered rather ungracefully down a rope-ladder and were bundled aboard with whispered curses by the French oarsmen. De Craon, accompanied by a number of soldiers dressed in half-armour, came up to greet them. 'Sir James Selkirk,' he said. 'Why such concern? What is the problem? Our master, King Philip IV, will not be pleased with the news that his ships cannot enter and leave the ports of Scotland without hindrance!' 'There is no hindrance!' Selkirk retorted. 'We simply wish to have a conversation with you and you have agreed. You know Master Corbett, the English envoy?' De Craon gave the sketchiest of bows. 'I think everyone knows Master Corbett!' he replied, 'with his eternal questions and his ability to stick his nose into matters which do not concern him. What is it this time, English Clerk?' 'His Grace, the Bishop of Glasgow,' Corbett replied, 'has asked me to request an audience with the Lady Yolande in order to clarify certain matters regarding the death of her late husband, King Alexander III of Scotland.' 'Certain matters!' de Craon snapped. 'I know your meddling, clerk! You came to Kinghorn and the Queen graciously granted you an audience during which you disturbed her. However, on the second occasion, she refused to see you and she will not see you now!'

Corbett stared at the hard-eyed French envoy and realised that it was impossible to press the matter. The galley was well-armed and it was unlikely that Sir James would give any assistance. Consequently, he was rather surprised when Selkirk spoke out. 'Monsieur de Craon,' he said. 'Your ship is in our waters, the Lady Yolande was married to a Scottish King. We bear warrants from the Council of Guardians of Scotland and yet you ignore us. If you wish, go on your way, but we shall report your rudeness and obduracy to Philip IV of France, who would not be too pleased to see future delicate negotiations hindered by the ill-manners of one of his envoys.' Selkirk stopped speaking and Corbett saw de Craon flinch at what the Scotsman had said as he quickly assessed the alternatives open to him. 'Monsieur de Craon,' Corbett said tactfully. 'I assure you that I will not give any offence to the Lady Yolande. I beg you to allow me to speak to her for a few moments, and, if you would be so kind, also to yourself. In confidence,' he concluded. 'It will be in confidence, I assure you, and no affront will be given.' De Craon stared bleakly at the English clerk and shrugged to show his unease. 'Very well,' he muttered. 'You may see Lady Yolande, not,' he lifted a warning finger, 'not in her cabin! I suggest that a few moments here on deck will suffice.' Corbett agreed and de Craon disappeared for a while.

The clerk heard voices raised in French and knew that Lady Yolande was protesting loudly at having to meet him. Nevertheless, de Craon's diplomatic skills prevailed and the Lady Yolande, a beautiful figure swathed in costly furs, came on deck and haughtily beckoned Corbett to her side. Corbett smiled wanly at Selkirk, nodded his thanks and walked over to join her. The arrogant princess refused to talk in English and Corbett had to use all his skill in French to conduct a conversation whilst ensuring he did not give offence. 'My Lady,' he began. 'I have simply one question to ask of you and, before you answer, I must inform you that I know full well the delicate details of your personal relationship with the late King.' He watched the woman's eyes widen in surprise. 'I assure you,' Corbett added hastily, 'simply one question.' 'Continue!' she commented tersely. 'Ask me the question! Let us have the matter done with!' 'On the night the King died,' Corbett replied, 'a message came saying that the King, would arrive at Kinghorn. So you expected the King?' Yolande nodded, watching Corbett closely. 'Well,' Corbett continued, 'the King did not arrive but Patrick Seton, the body-squire did. Surely you were concerned that your husband did not follow him? You must have thought that there had been an accident? And, if so, why did you not send Seton back to search for his master or send members of your own household to look for him?' 'Quite simply,' the French princess answered, 'Seton arrived at Kinghorn. I never liked him and I knew he hated me. I dismissed him as quickly as I could and later found that he had gone to drink himself into a drunken stupor. As for the King,' she edged closer to Corbett so only he could hear, her sweet cloying perfume catching his nostrils, until he almost thought that she was going to kiss him. 'As for the King,' the Princess hissed. 'I detested him. I hated his drunken ways, his many mistresses, his hard, scarred body. I could not have cared if he had been lying out on those wild moors bleeding to death. Do you understand me, English Clerk? I could not care! I was not concerned! Now, go!' Corbett, surprised by the venom and malicious hatred in the woman's eyes, hurriedly stepped away and watched as Yolande swirled off to her cabin. Corbett looked back across the galley to where Selkirk and de Craon were standing near the far ship rail. 'You have finished, Master Corbett?' de Craon called out sweetly, as if he was almost sorry at the reception the English clerk had received. 'I have finished, but I do have questions for you, Monsieur de Craon.' 'Then ask your damned questions,' de Craon snarled. 'For God's sake, ask them and let us go!' Corbett walked across and was grateful when Selkirk diplomatically moved out of earshot. 'Your questions, Monsieur?' de Craon tartly observed. 'They are ready?' 'Yes,' Corbett bluntly replied. 'Did the late King ever discuss his marriage with you?' 'What business is it of yours?' de Craon heatedly replied. 'The talks between a French envoy and a Scottish monarch are hardly a matter for an envoy of King Edward of England!' Corbett sensed he would make little progress if de Craon continued in this vein; he walked over to where a small, wooden crucifix was nailed to the mast and put his hand on it. 'I swear,' Corbett said emphatically, 'that my intention is not to spy for the English King. I swear this by the cross. I also swear that what I do is done with the full knowledge of Bishop Wishart!' Corbett crossed back to the envoy. 'Monsieur de Craon,' he urged. 'I speak the truth. I realise the Lady Yolande is a noblewoman and that you were instrumental in arranging her marriage to the late King. However, I also know that the marriage, because of the Lady Yolande, was never consummated.'

The French envoy started, ready to play the outraged courtier, but Corbett's steady gaze quietened him. He shuffled his feet and pursed his lips, trying to conceal his embarrassment and surprise at this dangerous, clever English clerk. De Craon shrugged and smiled, secretly wishing he had killed this man and vowing he would, the next time an opportunity presented itself. On his part, Corbett shrewdly watched the Frenchman and knew he was correct and so moved to close the trap.

'Did you discuss the Lady Yolande with King Alexander at the Council meeting the evening before he died?'

'Hardly, in the company of others!' 'Whom did the King talk to?' 'The Lord Bruce, Bishop Wishart, his esquires, Seton and Erceldoun, Benstede,' the last name was spat out. 'But you did spend the previous day with the King?' 'Yes,' answered de Craon surlily. Corbett now closed the trap, trying hard to control his excitement. 'Was it then you discussed a possible marriage with Lady Margaret, sister of Philip IV of France?' De Craon drew himself up. 'Sir!' he exclaimed. 'You go too far. It is none of your business! The Lady Margaret is a princess of the blood. You are not fit ...' He broke off suddenly, stared at Corbett and smiled coldly. 'That was good, Monsieur,' he muttered. 'Very clever. You are a good clerk, Monsieur Corbett.' He walked away, across the deck. 'Too good for this world, Monsieur! Au revoir.' 'I am sure we will meet again,' murmured Corbett but the Frenchman was out of earshot, shouting at his retainers and crew to make ready.

Without further ado Corbett, Selkirk and their small party returned to their own vessel. The galley pulled away, its oars dipping as it made its way down, following the tide out into the open sea. Their return to Leith on the "Saint Andrew" was just as uncomfortable as the journey out and Corbett was only too pleased to feel the firm ground of the quayside beneath him. Selkirk, however, was impatient to return. They collected their horses from the stables and were soon pounding their way back up the cobbled streets of Edinburgh to the Abbey of Holy Rood. Selkirk promised to leave his customary token force and Corbett, grateful for Selkirk's intervention and assistance on the French galley, began to thank the rather taciturn Scottish knight. 'Don't thank me,' Sir James replied. 'The sooner this business is done, Master Clerk, the sooner you are gone and that will make me very happy!' Corbett could only nod and turned to lead his horse from the abbey gates, when Selkirk called out, 'Mind you, Corbett, for an English clerk, you have some good qualities, and that is praise indeed from a Scotsman!' Corbett grinned his acknowledgement and continued into the abbey, pleased that the journey was done and the information he had received so helpful.

The Prior joined him in his small chamber, his sandalled feet beating like a tambour along the stone corridor, his grey gown billowing around him. 'Your sea journey was profitable?' the Prior observed. 'Did de Craon assist you?' Corbett smiled. 'De Craon's an excitable man,' he replied, 'and a bit of a fool. I tricked him, but I had to, I remember once seeing a mosaic, a Roman mosaic. Have you seen one?' The Prior shook his head. 'Well,' Corbett continued, 'it was beautiful. A woman's face, dark and mysterious with long, flowing black hair. The craftsman had created this vision with small, coloured stones, and some of them had come loose. I spent an entire day putting them back, watching that face, hundreds of years old, come to life.' He sighed. 'But painting and sculpture are not your interests. Surely, you are more concerned with herbs, drugs and poison?' He watched the Prior's sallow face flush. 'I am sorry, Father,' Corbett grinned. 'I wanted to shock you. I am like the painter of that mosaic, the small pieces are falling into place and I need your help. Tell me, is there any herb which will make you see images and, at the same time, sharpen your memory?' He then outlined to the Prior his experience in Ettrick Forest when he visited the Pictish village. The Prior, solemn-faced, heard him out. 'There are,' he replied, 'certain plants which cut, distilled and treated, can turn a man's mind and raise phantasms in his soul; the deadly nightshade, the purple foxglove, above all the flowers of Hecate, Queen of the Night, the black hellebore. Buttered almonds, or even the chewed leaves of the laurel. All of these can excite the mind, bring back lost memories.' He looked sharply at Corbett, his tired, clever eyes searching the English clerk's face. 'But you mentioned poisons, Hugh,' he added calmly, 'and all the plants I have mentioned could kill a man, choke out his life like a breeze snuffs out a candle.'

Corbett leaned forward and described what he had seen. The Prior questioned him closely and Corbett answered as accurately as he could. The Prior stopped speaking, thought and offered his conclusion. Corbett smiled slowly, the last stone was in place, the picture was complete and, in his mind's eye, he saw full and clear the face of the murderer of Erceldoun, Seton, the young man in his own retinue, the boatman and, above all, the regicide, the slayer of the Lord's anointed, King Alexander III of Scotland. Corbett asked the Prior one last favour, one more task, the monk agreed and slipped quietly out of the room.

SEVENTEEN

Corbett was at the dawn Mass the next day. He knelt and watched the priest offer the white body of Christ, the host and chalice lifted high, asking the Lamb of God to take away the sins of the world. Corbett took the sacrament, wishing to draw on its strength to combat the evil he would encounter that day. After Mass, he sent a last envoy south with a verbal message to be delivered to no one except the Chancellor of England, Robert Burnell, Bishop of Bath and Wells. The Chancellor, Corbett insisted, would be at Tynemouth Priory. If he was not, then the messenger was to wait until he arrived. Corbett then gave certain instructions to the Prior and Selkirk's armed escort, still on guard outside the abbey gates, and went back to his small cell.

Just before noon he heard voices in the passageway outside, leather boots rapping on the paved stones. There was a knock and Benstede walked in, smiling affably as he patted Corbett on the shoulder and stared around the bleak cell. 'Well,' Benstede said as soon as he had settled himself comfortably. 'You asked to see me?' Corbett nodded. 'I have found out who murdered King Alexander III, and how, but not the reason why.' For the first time since he had met him, Corbett saw genuine fear and shock in Benstede's face. The colour drained from his cheeks, the eyes lost their quizzical humorous look, his mouth sagged open. 'Who is it?' he whispered hoarsely. 'Why, Master Benstede,' Corbett replied. 'You know who it is. You are the murderer of Alexander III!' For a long while Benstede just sat and stared at Corbett. 'You cannot possibly ...' he began and then gulped. 'You have no proof. You are simply putting the blame on me, when it should be laid at the door of de Craon and his group of assassins.' Corbett watched Benstede's hand edge closer to the knife he kept in his belt. 'Master Benstede!' he snapped. 'I suggest that you keep your hand well away from your dagger and attempt no violence, cry out or try to summon assistance from that evil shadow who goes everywhere with you. He is probably as guilty as you are of at least four murders in Scotland. Yes,' Corbett continued. 'You are correct on a number of matters. The proof I have is tenuous and even if I caught you red-handed, I doubt if any Scottish court would dare try you. I am simply telling you because I believe I should, justice demands it. It is also in your interest to sit and listen quietly to what I am going to say.' Corbett rose and walked about the cell as he talked. 'In 1278,' he began, 'Alexander III attended the coronation of our Sovereign Lord, King Edward of England. He was asked to pay homage for his lands in England, to which he quickly agreed but stoutly refused to perform fealty for the realm of Scotland, claiming he held that direct of God. Our Master the King has, in the last fourteen years, developed the vision of his rule, the like of which has never been seen in this country since the days of the Roman Empire. He lays claim to vast lands in France. He has conquered Wales, crushed opposition at home, has designs on Ireland and, as he proved at his coronation, has similar plans for the kingdom of Scotland. I am not saying,' Corbett added hastily, 'that our Sovereign Lord was involved in, or even ordered, the death of King Alexander, but you, Master Benstede, are his faithful servant. You know his mind, his secret desires and wishes,' Corbett said. 'You are very similar to the knights who murdered Thomas à Becket at Canterbury. They did that of their own accord. Henry Angevin did not order them but Becket's death was the secret desire of his soul.' Corbett paused to gulp some wine before continuing. 'I believe Edward sent you to Scotland to see what you could accomplish in advancing his claims. After all, Alexander's heirs were all dead, his English wife was ten years in her grave and the King himself was advancing in years. If Alexander died without an heir then it would certainly give our King the necessary room to manoeuvre. However, Alexander changed all this. He began secret negotiations with the French and then compounded his sin by marrying a young French princess. For Edward this was serious: Alexander was married. He could well live a good score years and beget healthy sons to succeed him. Moreover, these sons would be half French and for the first time ever the Capetian monarchy would have client kings on Edward's own doorstep. I suspect that Alexander hoped for closer ties with France and these were the subject of his long detailed and secret discussions with de Craon. So you decided to act. Alexander was notorious for the complete disregard he had of his own life and limb, charging around Scotland in all weathers and despite all hazards. It would be easy for an accident to befall such a monarch, especially as he was a king who, after a long and successful reign, had little reason to fear enemies and so his escort was often no more than two men. Then, I suppose, you were given an opportunity. The Princess Yolande would not agree to consummating her marriage to Alexander. For what reason, neither you nor I really know, but the young princess's refusal provided you with a plan. You probably asked Seton to persuade the King to convoke the Council late in the afternoon of March 18th. The reason for the Council was petty enough, the imprisonment of a Scottish baron in England. Alexander was probably bored and only too willing to hold a meeting which might free one of his subjects, especially as the discussion was suggested by no less a person than Edward's envoy in Scotland. At the Council meeting you took Alexander aside with the important news that Queen Yolande urgently wanted to see him that night, sent her excuses for her recent bad behaviour and urged the king to join her the same day at Kinghorn.' Benstede snorted with laughter. 'But that is ridiculous,' he interjected. 'I would be the last person Queen Yolande would confide in.' 'Yes, I agree,' answered Corbett. 'But you did visit her the day before the Council meeting. You probably extended diplomatic courtesies. The Queen would say something which you later enhanced into a loving, intimate invitation. If your plan went awry you could always claim that it was the Queen who had misinformed you and so exacerbate Alexander's rage and frustration against her. You see, I know from the King's own confessor, Father John, that Alexander was so tired of his Queen's petulant protests and refusals that he was considering sending this confessor to Rome to ask the Pope for an annulment of his marriage on the grounds of non-consummation and permission to marry again, this time another French princess who might be more accommodating. You may have even known of this. I suspect you did and so time was of the essence. You gave the invitation to the King, asked him to keep the matter private and urged him to leave the Council as soon as possible for Kinghorn Ness. Meanwhile you had already left, accompanied by that misbegotten servant of yours.

You travelled to Queensferry but did not ask the ferryman to take you across the Forth. You asked the other man, the one you had deceived into believing you were French. He rowed you across in the storm, landed you at a secret place where you had horses already tethered and you rode through the night to the top of Kinghorn Ness. There, just where the plateau dips towards the beach, you fastened a rope and took your place across the path in some bushes. It must have been a long, cold and wet wait but eventually the King appeared.' 'This is nonsense!' interrupted Benstede. 'How was I to know that the King would come without an escort? How was I to see him in the dark? How could I distinguish him from any of his retinue?' 'Oh, that was quite simple,' replied Corbett. 'It would be dark on any March night on the top of Kinghorn Ness, that a violent storm was raging was an added advantage. As for the King's escort? You knew only too well Alexander's habits and ways. At the very utmost he would take two or even three men with him. One squire did actually pass the place, Patrick Seton, but his horse did not stumble across your trap because the rope lay slack upon the ground. When the King appeared, riding at breakneck speed, you or your servant, Aaron, jerked the rope up. The horse, galloping so quickly, simply stumbled and fell over the edge of the precipice taking the King with him.' Corbett took a deep breath and peered out of the cell's one and only narrow slit window. 'Of course,' Corbett continued, 'it would be easy for you to see the King. He was riding through the black night but his horse was white. You made sure that the horse the purveyor brought to the port of Inverkeithing was light-coloured.' 'And how did I manage that?' Benstede mocked. 'I have no authority to issue orders to members of King Alexander's household.' 'Oh, you are right,' Corbett retorted. 'But you used the other ferryman,

Taggart, to take you across the Forth. He thought you were a Frenchman and you used this disguise to make preparations on the other side of the Firth. On the morning of the 18th March I know that Taggart took you, still posing as a Frenchman, across to Kinghorn, but no Frenchman arrived at the manor. Instead an anonymous courier delivered a message saying the King was preparing to come there and the purveyor was instructed to bring down the King's favourite white mare, Tamesin, to Inverkeithing.' 'But the letter!' Benstede interrupted. 'I could not forge that.' His voice trailed off as he realised his mistake. 'I never said anything about a letter,' Corbett quickly replied, 'but, yes, a letter was sent, a forgery, no real feat for a trained clerk. I suspect you or Aaron delivered it at the royal manor gate. Anyway,' Corbett continued, 'you ensured the white mare, Tamesin, was brought down. On such a mount the King would be an easy target against the dark sky. Once the King had fallen, you unfastened the rope and slipped back to where your ferry was waiting for you. Taggart then rowed you back and, once his task was finished, you murdered him, the two of you together holding his head beneath the water until he drowned. After which, you beached and tied up his craft to look as if he had never left in the first place, and returned to Edinburgh. In the consequent confusion which broke out the following morning no one would notice your comings and goings.' Corbett noticed that Benstede was nervously biting his lower lip. 'There was no reason,' Corbett continued, 'for anyone to suspect you. You were probably elated at the news that Erceldoun had got lost in the storm but became alarmed when Seton began to mumble about shadows on Kinghorn Ness. Perhaps the young man had seen something? Perhaps he might recover and start asking questions or making statements? So you murdered him!' 'How,' Benstede almost shouted. 'How could I murder him? He never left his room! There was no mark of violence found upon his corpse!' 'You sent him presents,' replied Corbett, 'apples and a pair of gloves.' 'You are not saying that the food was poisoned, are you?' Benstede jibed. 'I know,' Corbett replied, 'the fruit was wholesome. Erceldoun probably ate more of the apples than Seton ever did. It was the gloves which were poisoned. You sent them as a gift but you are a doctor, Master Benstede. You told me so yourself. You know about herbs, poisons and their antidotes from your studies at Salerno in Italy. You simply had the gloves coated with a deadly poison, and waited for Seton to wear them.' 'A sick man!' screeched Benstede. 'Wearing gloves!' 'A bored, ill man,' replied Corbett. 'He would at least try them on. Handle them. You or your servant, Aaron, would have made sure of that when you visited him.' 'So where are these gloves?' jibed Benstede. 'Oh, you made sure they disappeared,' Corbett replied. 'I looked at the list of goods and chattels belonging to Seton. There was no mention of any gloves. I am sure you had them removed. The rest is quite simple,' Corbett continued. 'The poison was transferred to Seton's fingers and, when he ate, the poison acted quickly. You are right to say that poison leaves little trace upon a body but it does halt the corruption of the corpse and I noticed this when I opened Seton's tomb in St. Giles' graveyard. Of course,' Corbett said emphatically, 'you wanted to remove any interference in your plan and that included me. When I arrived in Edinburgh you immediately became suspicious, so you showed me the draft of your letter to King Edward. You wanted to find out if the King had sent me, that is why you told him about me. If I had objected to such an innocuous statement then you would have had immediate satisfaction. Even so, the

King would be curious and puzzled and probably order Burnell to recall me. As matters stand, I suspect the Chancellor has intercepted your letter and, if Edward ever gets to know that I am in Scotland, Burnell will fabricate some acceptable and reasonable explanation. Naturally,' Corbett added, 'you were alarmed at my interest in Alexander's death, so you brought along that old fool of a royal physician, MacAirth. He had examined the royal corpse and found nothing amiss. You thought he would calm all my anxieties. Of course he did not. The old fool, carried away by his own arrogance and a skinful of wine, babbled on and left me more curious. Even so, before this happened, you had already decided I was too dangerous. The night the Council held a banquet in the main hall of the castle, you, or Aaron, used the fight which broke out there as a cover to assassinate me. You have never taken a drug, I suspect, and neither have I, Master Benstede, until I arrived in Scotland.' Corbett looked at Benstede's pasty face but continued remorselessly. 'I was given a drug miles away from here but in a place you might feel at home in. Under its influence, I remembered standing by the pillar at that banquet and seeing Aaron glaring at me through the crowd, I now know he tried to kill me and when you saw me talking to Erceldoun, you decided he would have to die as well. Just as you tried to kill me on four occasions.' 'That is preposterous!' broke in Benstede. 'Erceldoun was a soldier. He was strangled, garrotted in St. Giles Church! No one would suspect me of having the strength to kill such a man, even if you imply that Aaron was my accomplice!' 'Oh, you are right,' Corbett smilingly replied. 'The coroner's report stated that Erceldoun was going down to St. Giles to see a priest. You are that priest, Master Benstede. A good friend of the late Patrick Seton, Erceldoun would not expect to meet his death at your hands. That wretched man entered the church of St. Giles and you were awaiting him at the entrance to the chancel. You possibly suggested that you wished to talk to him about the events on Kinghorn Ness? Perhaps a prayer for the late King or for the unfortunate Patrick Seton? Erceldoun would kneel, close his eyes, you would begin to pray aloud while you slipped the garrotte round his neck. It would not take you long. When I opened his grave I inspected the weal round his neck and saw the indentations caused by the very cord you now wear round your waist!' Benstede looked down in surprise and nervously fingered the knotted, tasselled cord round his middle. 'Very few people,' remarked Corbett, 'wear such a cord with similar knots. I noticed it the night of the banquet. You used that on Thomas Erceldoun and it left its own unique imprint upon his throat.' Corbett looked at Benstede, who was beginning to regain his composure as he realised the Scots could do little whilst he answered to no one except the English king. 'Really, Master Corbett,' he said softly, 'the only person who should have died was you with your searching questions and inquisitive ways.' 'You certainly tried,' Corbett tartly replied. 'In fact your attempts, or rather one of them, convinced me of your guilt. The dagger thrown in the hall could have been an accident or the work of the French.The attack on the road from Leith and later near Dalmeny Ford might also have been the work of outlaws, the French or the Bruce faction. But the same could not be said about the crossbow bolt which nearly shattered my head as I returned to the abbey the day after the banquet at the castle. It was too well-planned to be an outlaw attack. I had as yet not met the Lord Bruce, so the logical conclusion was that it was the French.' Corbett smiled at Benstede. 'Or rather that is what you hoped I would think after the attack failed.

When I left the castle you had me followed and subsequently I was detained by de Craon. Of course, the meeting was not amicable and the French might have pursued me. They did not. I went back to that dingy tavern and questioned the owner. I was fortunate for he informed me that de Craon and his companions never left that tavern until hours later. By which time, the attack was over and I was in the abbey. Oh, you were very clever, Master Benstede. You pointed me, as if I were some stupid dog, in a variety of directions – de Craon, Bruce, anyone who came to mind. You carried out those assassination attempts on me, protecting yourself by saying that you too were the object of assault. I am telling the truth, am I not?' Benstede rose, white-faced with fury. 'You don't understand,' he said. 'What I did, I did for the community of the realm of England. This country needs order, it needs laws, it is a threat to the security and well-being of our Sovereign Lord. Can you imagine a French princess upon the Scottish throne? Edward constantly turning and twirling to see from what direction the attack would come. You have heard of the new French king ordering marriage alliances for his children all over Europe. He intends to create an empire which would dwarf that of Charlemagne. What room would that leave for Edward? You have been through this country. You have seen the violence and how exposed our northern counties would be to such violence. It would be ten, twenty, thirty times worse if there was an alliance between the hostile French and the hostile Scots. If our King was in the south, the attack would be in the north and when he marched north the French would attack the channel coast. I did what I had to for the highest possible motives. If individuals die to save the lives of thousands, where is the wrong?' Corbett shook his head. 'Like me, Master Benstede, you have studied philosophy; evil means do not achieve a good end. Yes, I have seen this land. I agree that a hostile Scottish king would pose a serious threat to England's security but I have also seen the wild expanse of the country; the bogs, marshes, mountains and glens which would swallow England's armies and destroy them. But even if you are correct, Benstede, does this justify your actions? You murdered a good king, the Lord's anointed. You then murdered two young squires and are directly responsible for the violent death of an innocent young man in my retinue. While, in killing Taggart the ferryman, you destroyed a family. You are a murderer, Master Benstede, an assassin, and if there is a God in heaven you should answer for your crimes by the due process of law!' Benstede gathered his cloak about him and rose. 'I will answer to the King, the King of England, who is the fount of all law!' Benstede vehemently answered. 'The King will decide what is good and what is acceptable and then, Master Corbett, you narrow-minded, jumped-up clerk, we shall find out what the due process of law decides,' and, glaring at Corbett, Benstede opened the door and swept out. Corbett let him go, hearing his footsteps echo down the passageway before slumping, head in hands, on to his bed.

EIGHTEEN

Corbett felt drained, exhausted, but there was more to do. He took his cloak and walked slowly down the cloisters. 'Hugh?' a soft voice called. Corbett turned. The Prior anxiously searched the English clerk's white, drawn face. 'You have finished your task?' Corbett nodded. 'Is there anything I can do?' the monk asked. 'No, just tell Ranulf to join me in the stable courtyard.'

The ride to the castle was slow, Corbett made sure Selkirk's men fanned out around them. Here, in the city of Edinburgh, Corbett mused, he had to use the same tactics his commander had when advancing up a hostile valley in South Wales. He did not think Benstede would launch any attack but he felt it would be foolish not to take precautions. They clattered across the drawbridge into the castle. A servant fetched Selkirk, who crossly announced that the Bishop was reading his Office in the castle chapel. 'You will have to wait, Master Clerk!' he jibed. 'I think not!' Corbett replied and brushed him aside. The chapel lay at the back of the castle on the very summit of the great rock escarpment of Edinburgh. Corbett, followed by a panting, quietly cursing Ranulf, strode through the narrow, stone-vaulted castle corridors and up flights of stairs to the chapel. It was an ancient place, built by the saintly Queen Margaret, wife to Malcolm Conmore, the slayer of the tyrant Macbeth. It was also one of the smallest royal chapels Corbett had seen. Built of dark-grey stone, it must have only measured six yards long and four yards wide and consisted of a timber-roofed nave and a simply carved stone-vaulted apse, the two being separated by an archway. Under this knelt Bishop Wishart, praying before the bare wooden altar. He rose and turned as Corbett walked up the nave. 'Master Corbett, you could not wait?' he said softly. 'No, my Lord, I have waited long enough. The matter is finished.' Corbett turned as Ranulf, followed by Selkirk, entered the chapel. 'I would like to talk to you alone, my Lord.' The Bishop nodded at Sir James, who glared at Corbett but left, followed by a bemused Ranulf.

Wishart gestured to a bench alongside the far wall of the nave and they sat there, while Corbett summarised his conversation with Benstede, omitting any details he thought appropriate. The Bishop heard him out, concealing his surprise at this English clerk's stamina and logical brilliance. Corbett finished and Wishart rubbed his stubbled chin carefully, thinking out the consequences of what the clerk had told him. He pursed his lips and sighed. 'Benstede,' he admitted, 'did kill the late King but all the evidence you have mentioned could not be produced in court. It is a mixture of coincidence and careful calculation. Even if it was,' Wishart continued, 'it would cause uproar, threaten an already delicately-held peace.' He paused and stared fixedly at Corbett. 'Of course, I have not mentioned the reaction of your own master, King Edward of England. I accept that Benstede may have acted on his own initiative but I have my suspicions. If this matter were brought into the public eye, you would scarce receive the thanks of a grateful monarch. You could not return to England and you would not be welcome to stay here!' 'And Benstede?' Corbett interrupted bitterly. 'The regicide, the slayer of the Lord's anointed, not to mention the murderer of four men whose blood cries out for justice and vengeance.' 'Vengeance is mine, saith the Lord. I shall repay,' the Bishop replied soothingly, pleased to put the clerk down. 'Well, payment is long overdue!' Corbett tartly replied. The Bishop shifted uneasily on the hard wooden bench. 'It's not Benstede,' he snapped, 'who is dangerous. It's you, Master Corbett, with your search for the facts, your ability to ferret out the truth. The truth often hurts. It does no good, this turning over of stones. And why?' Wishart asked. 'What business is it of yours?' 'I do not know,' Corbett replied. 'I was given orders and I carried them out. Perhaps one day I will know the reason why!' 'But not here!' replied Wishart firmly. 'You will be gone, within forty-eight hours, you and all your retinue must be out of Edinburgh and journeying south to the border. If you are not, you will be arrested for treason!'

Corbett stood, his face now flushed with anger. 'You, especially, my Lord, want me gone. You know that I know the truth!' He almost jabbed a finger in the Bishop's face. 'You knew that the King was murdered. How? Why? And by whom? Perhaps not, but you still did nothing. Every time you looked at me you remembered your own guilt!' Wishart stood up and walked to the steps of the chancel, trying to control his temper. 'Yes,' he replied angrily. 'I knew but I had no proof, no evidence; even now I can do nothing! Nothing at all! Go now, Master Clerk!'

Corbett bowed and muttered something. 'What was that, Clerk?' Wishart snapped. 'A quotation from the Psalms, my Lord, "Put not your trust in Princes".' The Bishop sighed. 'Come back, Master Clerk! Come back! Look!' the Bishop edged closer to Corbett. 'I can do nothing. I hold Scotland from the brink of civil war. The King is dead, murdered, but he is dead. Yet,' he added bitterly, 'if a king of Scotland can suffer an accident then so can an English envoy. Rest assured, Benstede and his servant will never leave Scotland alive!' Wishart extended his hands as if in a blessing. 'What more can I do?' he said softly. 'Except give you an escort out of Scotland. 'Yes, there is something!' Corbett suddenly remembered the widow, Joan Taggart, surrounded by her hungry, frightened children. 'There is a woman, the widow of the boatman whom Benstede killed, she lives near Queensferry. Now she and her children starve.' 'You have my word,' the Bishop replied. 'They will be well looked after. Now!' he added briskly, 'you must be gone, Clerk, in forty-eight hours.' Corbett sketched a bow and left the old Bishop, the echoes of his steps ringing round the small, empty church.

The Prior and his monks were disconsolate at Corbett's abrupt departure. They had grown accustomed to his eccentric, secretive ways, his sudden and mysterious comings and goings, his help in the library and scriptorium. 'We shall miss you, Hugh,' the Prior said. 'We wish you a safe journey. I am sending two of my lay brothers with you, they will carry letters of safe conduct. No enemy, English or Scots, would dare attack a man under the protection of the Abbey of Holy Rood!' Corbett smiled and embraced the Prior, feeling his fragile, bony shoulders beneath the grey, fustian robe. 'What with your letters and Sir James's men, who undoubtedly await me beyond the abbey, I shall be safe.' Corbett clasped the Prior's hands, said his farewells and soon he, a relieved Ranulf and two lay brothers from the abbey, were clear of Edinburgh riding south-east for the border with England. Behind him, fanned out in a line like a long shadow were Sir James Selkirk's men, despatched to ensure the troublesome English clerk left Scotland for good.

Corbett travelled through the Lammermuir Hills, now in

their full summer glory. Oak trees, pines and beeches covered the hillsides and escarpments, whose flanks were scored and gouged by narrow, fish-filled streams. Corbett was content, at peace now he was leaving the dark intrigue of Edinburgh. He was conscious of the soldiers shadowing him but they kept their distance. Corbett travelled light and therefore fast. At night they sheltered under trees or in the byres and barns of solitary farms and shepherd-holdings. Four days after they left Edinburgh, their horses passed the dark mass of Berwick and splashed across the Tweed into England.

Beneath the huge, Norman keep of Norham Castle, built on a great crag above the river, Corbett said farewell to the lay brothers and made his way up the craggy promontory into the fortress. The Constable, a grizzled, wiry-haired soldier, was waiting for him in the outer bailey, with others wearing the livery of the Chancellor standing around him. 'Master Corbett, clerk to the King's Bench?' the man barked. 'The same,' Corbett replied, dismounting from his horse. 'The Chancellor is here?' 'Yes,' the Constable replied. 'He is waiting. Please follow me!' Corbett told Ranulf to make himself comfortable and followed the soldier up into the great keep.

Burnell, plump and wheezing, his soft, flabby hands constantly mopping his completely bald head, met him at the door of the castle's solar and, thanking the Constable, personally escorted Corbett into the gaunt, deserted room. It was a bleak granite, timber-roofed chamber dominated by a stone-built fireplace and long, oval-shaped windows. The furniture was scanty; a long oak table, heavy chairs like church benches and great iron-bound chests. There was a tray with a jug of wine and simple pewter cups on the table. Burnell filled two of them and beckoned to Corbett. 'Come, Hugh, it is good to see you. We will sit in the window-seat and catch the breezes. An ideal place from which you can watch both England and Scotland. You received my letters? I received yours,' he added, not waiting for a reply. Corbett sat and, at the Chancellor's invitation, told his master everything. He did not omit any details, he was not fooled by the fat, flabby bishop who sat alongside him, his razor-sharp mind would not miss anything. The Bishop, slurping his wine, let the clerk speak, interrupting now and again with the occasional terse question or comment. Outside, a linnet sang while it wheeled in its own splendour against the gold, sun-filled sky. Corbett stopped talking, watched it for a while and then quietly concluded. 'There is no more. So now, why was I sent there?' Burnell cleared his throat. 'First,' he replied, 'have no worries about Benstede. I know Bishop Wishart and I believe Benstede will never be allowed to leave Scotland alive. As for the Scots, I doubt very much whether you will ever set foot in their country again, while I will conceal your activities from His Grace. After all,' and Burnell smiled sourly, 'I have as much to lose as you, that is why I took such care to intercept any letters Benstede sent south for the King.'

Burnell stood up to ease the cramp from his body and walked slowly to and fro while Corbett sat and watched him. 'I sent you to Scotland,' Burnell began, 'without the King's authority and under my own commission because I do not want a war between England and Scotland. Both countries are at peace, both enjoy and profit from the calm. Edward our King has always thought different. He is a conqueror, Corbett; he has smashed the Welsh, killed their chieftains and turned their kingdoms into English shires dominated by his grey, heavy castles. He has always wanted to do the same with Scotland. First, he married his sister, Margaret, to Alexander III with the prospect that one of his nephews would sit on the Scottish throne,' Burnell paused before going on. 'Then, Margaret and the two boys died. Our King accepted that, though he tried unsuccessfully to wrest homage for Scotland from Alexander III. He wished to establish the principle of English supremacy over Scotland for that would come in useful if a nephew succeeded to the Scottish throne or if there was an uncertain succession. Anyway,' the Bishop continued wearily, 'Alexander, heirless, becomes the amorous bachelor. Our sovereign lord is quite content with that but then matters change. A new French King, Philip IV, ascends the throne with dreams grander than Edward's. Have you ever heard any of his lawyers speak or read their memoranda?' Corbett shook his head. 'They make fascinating reading,' the Bishop said meditatively and rejoined Corbett in the window-seat before continuing. 'They see Philip as a new Charlemagne and this alarms Edward. More so when Philip opens secret negotiations with Alexander and produces the beautiful Yolande for a wife. Now, it could be Philip's kinsman on the Scottish throne, so Edward sends the humble Benstede as his envoy to Scotland, not with precise orders, may I hasten to add, to kill Alexander. Oh no! Just verbal instructions "to do all within his power to block and impede the French alliance".' 'And Alexander is killed?' 'Yes,' Burnell replied. 'Then I became suspicious. If Alexander's death was an accident or a murder by someone else then so it is, but,' Burnell's voice rose, 'if it could be laid at Benstede's door then I know, whatever he may say, Edward's real long-term plans for Scotland!' 'But King Edward,' interrupted Corbett, 'has been most quiet in this matter!' 'Publicly,' Burnell replied, 'yes. Privately, no. I do think Edward's detachment from what is happening in Scotland is a mask. He did not murder Alexander but must be pleased that the Scottish King lies dead for it fulfils his own secret plans to annex the kingdom.

Burnell paused and looked hard at Corbett. 'I now know, because of your visit to Scotland, that Edward sent Benstede there as part of his grand design to annex that kingdom by peaceful means if necessary, but, if that fails, then by war.' 'But Edward has been in France?' queried Corbett, 'deeply involved in Gascony affairs.' 'He is,' Burnell smiled, 'but I do know from my spies in the Exchequer that the royal treasury clerks have despatched an interest-free loan of two hundred pounds sterling to Eric, King of Norway.' 'You mean?' Corbett exclaimed. 'Oh! There is more,' continued Burnell. 'Edward has also sent secret envoys to Rome asking for a papal dispensation for his two-year-old son to marry within the forbidden degrees of consanguinity. The bride has already been chosen for there are English envoys now in Norway attempting to secure the hand of the Princess Margaret in marriage for Edward's own son. So, you see, Master Corbett, the King has been most active in this Scottish matter. By fair means or foul, he intends to get his son on the Scottish throne!' 'Yet,' Corbett replied, 'if the Prince Edward does marry Margaret, it would mean a peaceful conclusion to the affair.' Burnell almost snorted in derision. 'For the love of the Sweet God and all his sons!' the Chancellor exclaimed. 'You have been in Scotland, Hugh. You have seen Wishart, the Bruce, the Scottish lords. Do you really think they will allow an English prince to wear the Scottish crown? Do you think Bruce will give it up like some nun who enters the convent and renounces all wealth? There is more. The Princess Margaret is only two, the same age as Edward's son. The Scottish court know it will be years before either succeeds to the throne and who would be their guardian?' Burnell smiled. 'No less a person than our sovereign dread lord, Edward of England, and he would not allow the grass to grow under his feet. English castles built. Scottish strongholds garrisoned with English troops. English barons, churchmen and clerks in positions of responsibility. No,' Burnell concluded. 'I have thought the matter out. The murder of Alexander III will only lead to the death of the Princess Margaret and the deaths of hundreds, maybe thousands, of English and Scots and in the end we will lose.' Corbett sat and thought about the visions he had seen in the Pictish village and the prophetic words of Thomas of Learmouth. 'Well,' Burnell said, rising to his feet. 'You did well, Hugh. the matter is now in my hands. You are to return immediately to London and resume your duties. I shall see you before you leave.'

The old Bishop, muttering to himself, shuffled out of the door. Corbett remained, looking out of the window. The sun had gone, a strong wind had arisen. He looked across the Tweed and saw the dark stormclouds gathering above Scotland. Images passed through his mind. Alexander III, King of Scotland, black against the night sky as he fell to his lonely death. Wishart, foxy eyes, the power and the fury of the Lord Bruce. Then, once again, the lines of Thomas of Learmouth passed through his mind and he knew the prophecy was right. The green hills below him would run with blood before the murder of Alexander III, the death of the Lord's anointed, was expunged from the face of the earth. His death would need atonement before his crown moved out of the gathering darkness.

NINETEEN

In Edinburgh Castle John Benstede, clerk and special emissary from Edward of England, was also drawing his affairs to a close. His baggage and trunks with their secret compartments for letters, memoranda, bills and items of business had been taken downstairs by Aaron and strapped on sumpter ponies waiting in the courtyard. Benstede looked round the cold stone-wall chamber. He had left nothing and was secretly pleased to be going. He had already visited Bishop Wishart to thank him for his hospitality and had been slightly surprised by the Bishop's effusive warmth. He was too friendly, thought Benstede, and wondered if the Bishop knew anything about Corbett's revelations.

Benstede slumped on to the straw-filled bed and, not for the first time, quietly cursed the inquisitive English clerk. He had heard about Corbett, a secretive, ambitious, ruthless man though, Benstede concluded, one with a conscience. Such a man should not be allowed to play a part in public affairs. There was a time for conscience but this did not apply to the important matters between kings and countries. Surely, Benstede thought, would it matter if a few men died so that peace could be maintained? And the good order Edward had established in England be spread as in Roman times throughout the entire land?

Benstede worshipped Edward. He saw the English king as a living reincarnation of all that was good and proper in a knight and in a king. Benstede had read the Arthurian romances spread by the minstrels and troubadours of France and England and considered that if they were true, then Edward was Arthur come again. The English king had brought peace and good order to Wales, built roads, stimulated trade, healed the wounds of civil war and, through his use of Parliaments, brought the whole kingdom and entire community of the realm into one coherent organisation. Benstede loved order and hated chaos. Everything had its place, everything should be ordered. Benstede was a doctor and had seen the ravages of sickness in the human body. As Saint Augustine said, "The kingdom was the body and there were diseases ever ready to break out, the pus and the evil humours spreading through every limb causing infection and bringing everything to nothing".

Scotland under the wrong king could be a bubo or growth on England. Time and again Edward had confided to Benstede his dreams about not only restoring the empire of Henry of Angevin but expanding it. Northern France was to be conquered, Wales and Ireland annexed and Scotland subjugated. The empire of the mysterious Arthur was to be re-established in harmonious union under one ruler. Edward paid particular attention to Scotland, pointing out that the northern kingdom was the greatest threat to his realm. A hostile Scotland could bring war and devastation to England's northern shires with their long exposed borders and vulnerable coastlines. In 1278 Edward tried to force Alexander to concede that the English king was his overlord. Alexander refused and publicly insulted Edward, who never forgave or forgot such a gesture. Nevertheless, the English king was patient.

He had worked too hard to lose Scotland, sacrificing his own dear sister to gain it only to see his nephews, Alexander's sons, die in mysterious circumstances. Edward had often wondered, in Benstede's company, if the boys had actually been killed by the French or factions hostile to England. Nonetheless, Edward was satisfied that the Scottish king was childless for if he died without an heir Edward would advance his claims by arranging a marriage between his own baby son and Margaret, the Maid of Norway, and so the English king's writ would run from Cornwall to the northernmost tip of Scotland. There would be no more raids, no more wars along the northern march, no danger of a foreign king or prince using Scotland as a postern-gate into England.

Edward hoped this would happen but Alexander and the interfering, conniving King Phillip of France proved they wished to change all this. English spies in Scotland reported an increase in envoys from Paris and the English were horrified to learn that Philip had managed to persuade Alexander to marry the spoilt bitch Yolande. Edward, fearing the worst, immediately despatched Benstede to Scotland to see what might happen. At first, Benstede believed he could do nothing but simply watch and report to his master: he had considered a secret alliance between Edward and the Bruce faction but realised that, ambitious as the Bruces were, they would never plot against the Scottish king just to hand the crown to Edward. Consequently, Benstede diverted his attention to Alexander III and his new queen and hardly believed his good fortune to discover that relations between the king and his new bride were far from harmonious. Benstede would have let matters stay like that, or even secretively encouraged the Scottish King's break from his wife, helping him to obtain a decree of divorce from the

Pope on grounds of non-consummation. That would have taken years. The Pope was in the hands of the French and would not quickly allow an annulment which would certainly insult the French court. Yet, once again, Alexander had moved quickly and secretively. Urged on by the devious and sinister de Craon, Alexander, so Benstede discovered, not only intended to divorce Yolande but immediately marry Margaret, the sister of Philip IV, and so move Scotland completely under French influence. The papacy, far from delaying the annulment would, under French pressure, actually hasten it through in a matter of months. Of course, Benstede was angry and the red-faced, boisterous Alexander had often teased Edward's envoy with malicious relish, baiting and taunting him with the prospects of a French prince sitting on the ancient throne of Scone. 'What then?' he had once jibed at Benstede. 'How does this fit in with your master's grand design? Never again, Master Benstede,' he shouted, 'will an English king demand from a Scottish monarch fealty for his own kingdom. Do you understand that? If you do, tell your master. Never, I repeat, never!' It was after such an interview that Benstede had decided Alexander must die, for what the Scottish king intended would plunge most of Europe into a bitter war and Edward would see his dreams fade. 'No,' Benstede whispered to himself, 'Alexander deserved to die.' The English envoy smiled to himself. It had all been so easy. The humble approach to an attentive ear, the quiet careful planning. A visit to Kinghorn, then back to Edinburgh to inform the King that his proud, pouting wife was aflame with desire for him. Other preparations were made. He had used that boatman, Taggart, to transport supplies across to caves on the other side of the Forth whilst Aaron had gone deeper into the countryside and purchased horses to stable there.

After that, everything had gone to plan, even the storm was in his favour. Once Alexander attended the Council meeting, Benstede gave him the false message from his wife and promptly journeyed across the Forth to join Aaron, who had delivered a letter at Kinghorn, saying the King was to be there later that night and ordering the purveyor to bring the King's favourite horse down to the ferry. Together, he and Aaron had placed thin ropes across the cliff-top path and the King on his white horse showed up clear as any target against the night sky. The ruse had been most effective. Benstede had seen English troops in Wales use similar methods in the narrow, Welsh valleys to bring down enemy horsemen or trip the unwary messenger. Of course, the two squires had posed problems. Seton's sharp eyes must have noticed or seen something. What, Benstede never established. So, he too, had to die and Erceldoun with him. Everything was in order, that is, until Corbett arrived. Benstede ground his teeth: clever, cunning Corbett with his soft, narrow, studious face and innocent questions. Benstede could hardly believe that the fellow had had the tenacity and intelligence to see through his schemes and unravel them.

At first, Corbett's revelations had made Benstede panic but then his cool, logical mind began to analyse events. Whom could Corbett tell? Burnell? He was the King's minister and would do what the King required. The Scots? But who would be displeased at Alexander's sudden demise? Bruce, hungry for the throne, or Wishart who was never liked or trusted by the dead King? And how could Corbett prove it? 'He has nothing,' Benstede murmured to himself. 'Nothing at all. All shadows and no substance. Some smoke but no fire.'

Benstede pursed his lips in satisfaction and rose to his feet at the clamour from the courtyard below. He looked through the narrow, arrow-slit window and saw Aaron patiently waiting, holding the reins of the two sumpter ponies and horses which would take them back to Carlisle where he would use his warrants to commandeer a fast ship to France. He would tell Edward everything that had happened. He knew the King would surely understand. Benstede noticed the noise which had disturbed him came from two boys playing with wooden swords outside the stables. One, a black-haired urchin, the other he recognised as the Earl of Carrick's grandson, young Robert Bruce. He watched the tousled, red-haired boy feint and parry like some dancer as he wielded his wooden sword and drove with shouts and jeers his poor opponent into a heap of horse-dung piled high in the courtyard corner. Benstede, happy and content with the world, shouted, 'Well done! Well done, boy!' dug into his purse and sent a silver coin twinkling down into the courtyard. The boy pushed his hair back, squinted up at the castle window and slowly walked over to where the silver coin had fallen, picked it up and tossed it to his defeated companion. He did not even acknowledge Benstede's gift but sauntered arrogantly away. 'The proud young cock!' Benstede muttered to himself. 'He and his family with their aspirations and dreams of the crown and royalty!' Benstede grinned, satisfied that Bruce's dreams would never be realised and, taking one last look round the room, carefully made his way down the winding stone staircase.

The horses were saddled and he and the silent Aaron were soon clattering across the drawbridge. A solitary knight was waiting for them and Benstede recognised Sir James Selkirk, Wishart's man and the captain of that prelate's household. 'Why, Sir James,' Benstede remarked. 'Have you come to see us off? Or do you bear messages from your master?' Selkirk slowly shook his head.

'Certainly not, Master John. I am simply making my way back into the castle, though I understand from His Grace, Bishop Wishart, that you are leaving Scotland today!' 'Well, not today,' Benstede jovially replied. 'It will take us at least three days hard riding to reach the border. You must be glad that we are going.' 'Visitors from England,' Selkirk quietly replied, 'are always welcome. Your countryman, Master Hugh Corbett, is already on his way. I bid you adieu!' Benstede nodded, dug the spurs into his horse, and clattered on his journey.

They bypassed Edinburgh and were soon into the soft countryside, making their way south-west to the border and security of Carlisle Castle. A beautiful summer's day, the strong sun's rays striking like a blade through the canopy of trees as the countryside slept in the summer haze. Towards evening they found themselves still in open country so Benstede decided that they must camp and indicated a copse of trees in the far distance. 'We will stay there,' he told his silent companion. 'We will eat, sleep and continue our journey tomorrow.' Benstede repeated what he had said with deft, smooth signals of his fingers and Aaron nodded. They approached the copse and followed the path as it narrowed into a hollow, splashing through the reedy shallows of a small stream and disturbing the blue dragonflies which hung there still enjoying the warmth of the dying sun. Benstede went further on, stopped and looked round for a suitable place to camp.

Satisfied with the day's journey, Benstede lifted the wineskin from his saddle and, pulling back the stopper, raised it up so its sweet contents splattered into his parched mouth. A crossbow bolt thudded into his exposed chest. Benstede lowered the wineskin slowly and coughed in surprise as both wine and blood dribbled from his mouth. He turned and looked for Aaron but his silent companion was already dead, a second crossbow bolt taking him full in the throat. Benstede slumped like a drunken dreamer from his saddle, the wineskin falling from his hand and the red wine spluttering in circles on the ground as it mixed with the blood pouring from both his mouth and chest. A bird whistled overhead and the dying man almost answered it with the bubbles breaking in his own throat. The smell of crushed grass tickled his nostrils as Benstede wondered what was happening to him. 'Corbett!' he thought. 'Corbett was responsible.' He had made, Benstede reflected in his dying moments, the most serious mistake of his life. He had trusted Corbett. He thought Corbett knew the rules. Nevertheless, Benstede comforted himself, he had done what he had to do. His agents in the Norwegian court in Oslo already had their instructions. It would all be well in the end. He felt the blood rise like a gorge in his throat as the darkness came quietly crashing round him.

In the shadows of the trees Sir James Selkirk carefully put down the huge crossbow he carried and, drawing his sword, walked soundlessly over to the prostrate figures. Aaron was dead, slumped like some sleeping child, face down on the earth. Benstede lay on his back, hands outstretched, lips still silently moving as his eyes glazed over. Selkirk stood and watched him die. 'You see, Master Benstede,' he murmured softly. 'I was right! You are leaving Scotland today!'

Selkirk looked around. He had followed both riders ever since they had left Edinburgh Castle. It had been easy. They had suspected nothing and so expected nothing. The knight had thought he would have to wait longer, but when he realised his quarry intended to sleep out in the open in a lonely Scotish wood, then he knew that such an opportunity could not be resisted. Selkirk walked silently back through the wood until he came to a small clearing hidden by a canopy of trees. The ground was soggy and easy to break up and, quickly digging a shallow grave, he dragged the bodies of both men into it. He also dug a small hole for the saddles and other baggage after he had rummaged through them for anything of value for himself or his master. The unsaddled horses and ponies were then pricked in the haunches and sent cantering into the gathering darkness. Selkirk was confident that they would find their way back to some farmstead or village where the local peasants would hardly believe their good fortune. Satisfied that all was done, Selkirk collected his own horse and made his way back to Edinburgh. Already he knew his master would be preparing the draft letter to Edward of England sadly answering Edward's expected enquiry on the "whereabouts of his envoy". After all, such accidents, as Wishart would caustically comment, were common occurrences in Scotland.

AUTHOR'S NOTE

The death of Alexander III occurred as described in these pages. The King and Queen Yolande were often apart and, on the evening of 18th March 1286, the King did announce, to the surprise of all his Council, that he intended to ride through a storm across the dangerous Firth of Forth and so reach Queen Yolande at Kinghorn Manor. The Council, convened to discuss the imprisonment of a Scottish baron, loudly objected and protested that the inclement weather was against such a journey. Alexander, however, persisted and his Councillors did not demur for Alexander's wild rides around Scotland were an accepted fact of life. The King left Edinburgh with two body-squires and crossed at Queensferry. Both the ferrymaster and the waiting purveyor, Alexander, did try to restrain the King but their protests were of no avail. The King began his wild ride into the fierce storm and fell to his death from Kinghorn Ness.

It is a matter of speculation whether the King's fall was an accident or murder. Many did stand to gain from his death. The Bruces and the Comyn faction ignored Bishop Wishart and eventually drifted into savage inter-clan rivalry. Edward of England continued to act as a mediator, though it is interesting that at the time of Alexander's death he arranged huge loans to the Norwegian king and had despatched envoys to the Pope to ask for papal permission for his young son to be betrothed to the Maid of Norway. Philip IV of France was also interested in Scottish affairs and continued to be so throughout his reign. Eventually Edward of England showed his hand. At first he acted as an honest broker between the rival Scottish claims to the throne, but then only supported the candidate who was prepared to accept his liegeship over Scotland. The Maid of Norway never reached Scotland but mysteriously died on the voyage over. This was the signal for the Bruce faction to advance their claims and a savage war between England and Scotland broke out which lasted decades and cost countless lives.

Many people believe that power politics between great nations is a development of the late 19th and early 20th centuries. This is not so. Edward I had very clear ideas about empire and conquests and Philip IV of France was no different. The latter too had dreams of obtaining an empire in Europe greater than Charlemagne. He regarded the Pope, who had fled to Avignon in Southern France, as simply an extension of his own influence. He married his sons and daughters off to the greatest nobles of Europe and later had a formal alliance with Scotland against England. Philip's political philosophy was expressed by one of his lawyers, Pierre du Bois, whose writings are still extant and prove fascinating reading. This constant clashing between the Plantagenets of England and the Capetians of France not only fuelled the war in Scotland but was one of the major causes for the later Hundred Years War which ranged from the Low Countries to Spain.

Thomas of Learmouth, or Thomas the Rhymer, is a historical figure. Some of his poetry is still extant. He did prophecy Alexander III's death and the consequent confusion which would follow. His prophecies proved only too accurate. Edward I died near Carlisle in 1307 still urging his heir (Prince Edward) and his barons to continue the war until they had achieved the ultimate victory but his successor and eldest son, King Edward II, proved unequal to the task. In 1314 one of the greatest English armies ever assembled during the medieval period was met by Robert Bruce at Bannockburn. The English army was disastrously defeated, the English king barely escaping with his life. In the words of Thomas the Rhymer – "The Bannockburn ran with blood".